CRANDALLS'
CASTLE

CRANDALLS' CASTLE

Betty Ren Wright

SCHOLASTIC INC.

New York Toronto London Auckland Sydney
Mexico City New Delhi Hong Kong Buenos Aires

ISBN 0-439-77771-2

Copyright © 2003 by Betty Ren Wright.
All rights reserved. Published by Scholastic Inc.,
557 Broadway, New York, NY 10012,
by arrangement with Holiday House, Inc. SCHOLASTIC and associated
logos are trademarks and/or registered trademarks of Scholastic Inc.

12 11 10 9 8 7 6 5 4 3   5 6 7 8 9 10/0

Printed in the U.S.A.   40
First Scholastic printing, April 2005

For Rebecca Draper and Rhoda Nathan,
my "honorary nieces"

CRANDALLS'
CASTLE

Chapter One
CHARLI

Charli Belland sat on the front steps and watched her Crandall cousins run happily wild around her. The four-year-old twins, Gene and Terry, were building a fort, using boxes and crates they'd dragged from the Belland garage. As soon as they completed a wall, they took turns riding their tricycles into it at full speed to batter it down. Two-year-old Mickey hurled toys out of his playpen in every direction.

"I cleaned up the whole yard this morning," Charli said grimly. "I wanted it to look nice when Mom and Ray come home."

Sixteen-year-old Dan, the only Crandall not in motion, laughed. "Why'd you bother?" he asked. "You knew we were all coming over for the big welcome home this afternoon. Aunt Rona knows what we're like, and Ray might as well get used to us. Every time he looks across the street at our yard he'll see a bigger mess than this."

Charli nodded. She considered getting up to collect the toys, but she didn't. Waiting like this, not knowing what was going to happen next, was pleasant. She felt as if her whole life was about to change.

"If you think this is bad, look out," Dan added. "I just found out we're getting a new kid in our family."

Charli looked up at him, startled.

"Not another baby," Dan told her with a grin. "It's a girl from Madison. She's related to someone my mom knows, and she has nowhere else to go. So . . ."

Charli understood. The girl in Madison had nowhere else to go, so of course Aunt Lilly had invited her to come and stay with the Crandalls. What difference would one more make?

"How old is she?"

"Fourteen," Dan said. "And that's all I've heard, so don't ask." He grinned. "You know my mother. Say yes and ask questions later—that's her motto."

He broke off as a familiar car turned onto Lincoln Street and glided to a stop in front of Charli's house. At the same moment, the screen door burst open and Uncle Will and Aunt Lilly rushed out onto the porch.

"Here they come!" Uncle Will shouted unnecessarily. "Welcome home, newlyweds!"

Charli stood up and started toward the car. She wanted to be cool, but her heart was banging in her chest. Uncle Will galloped ahead of her, and as soon as her mother and Ray Franz, her new stepfather, stepped from the car, he grabbed Charli's shoulders and swung her around to stand between them.

"Smile!" he shouted, raising his camera. "Let's see the happy family!"

The camera clicked, and then everyone hugged and shook hands, as if the honeymoon had lasted a lot longer than two days. A print glided out of the camera, and they crowded around to examine it. Charli saw that her mother and Ray were smiling happily, while she stared straight ahead, somber as an owl, through her round glasses.

"Charlene looks as if she's getting ready to run," Ray commented. "Is that the way it is, Charli?"

She glanced up at him, pretty sure he was teasing, but afraid he wasn't. "No," she said. "I'm staying." The whole family laughed, as if she'd said something clever instead of totally dumb.

Aunt Lilly threw one arm around Charli's mother and the other around Ray. "Come on inside your house," she ordered. "Dan, bring the suitcases. Charli and I spent all morning decorating the wedding cake."

"Cake!" Gene and Terry stampeded to the kitchen where the cake waited in all its glory on the table. When everyone had admired the rosebuds and plastic lovebirds, Rona and Ray together cut generous pieces and passed them out.

The littlest Crandalls took their paper plates and scattered around the backyard. Charli settled with Dan on the porch steps. He was four years older than she was and sometimes treated her as if she were a baby, but now he looked solemn, in spite of the frosting mustache that decorated his upper lip.

"Ray seems like an okay guy," he said. "I guess he's a good basketball coach—everybody says Mount Pleasant is lucky to get him. You like him, huh?"

"He's all right," Charli said. After all, she and her mom had been doing fine, just the two of them. She'd felt prickles of envy occasionally, when her friends at school mentioned their fathers, but she'd become used to having one parent. Her own father had died when she was three, and that had been that. At least, that was that until Ray came along.

She remembered the first evening he came to the house to take her mother out on a date. He had arrived in Mount Pleasant just a few days earlier to teach math and coach high school basketball. The morning he came to town to find a place to live and get settled, Rona Belland had served him coffee and pancakes at the Blue Water Café, where she was the manager. That was how they met.

"Do you like him?" her mother had asked the morning after the date.

"He's nothing like Uncle Will," Charli had said cautiously. Will Crandall, her mother's older brother, was the only man she knew really well. He had been an important part of her life ever since her father's death.

"No," her mother agreed. "Ray's nothing like our Will. They're both good and generous, but

Ray's a very different kind of person. For one thing he's steady as a rock. I hope you'll like him."

For the rest of that day Charli had felt uneasy and a little scared, but excited, too. Ray came over many evenings after that, filling a place in their lives that she hadn't realized was empty. Sometimes she'd wished he would disappear, but at the same time she'd practiced saying "my dad" when no one was around to hear.

"Your cake's slipping off the plate," Dan pointed out now. "Are you going to be Charli Belland or Charli Franz?"

"Who knows?" It would be nice if they all had the same last name, but she had been Charli Belland for a lot of years. She felt like Charli Belland.

The screen door burst open and Uncle Will bounded out onto the porch. He was like a puppy, Charli thought—if you could imagine a tall, skinny, gray-haired puppy. When he threw himself down onto the steps beside them and stretched out his long legs, he seemed younger than Dan.

"Listen up, kids," he whispered, pretending to check for eavesdroppers. "I've got a surprise! I don't want to tell you until everything's settled, but when I do you're going to be thrilled. Something terrific's coming off—great for us and maybe for Rona, too, Charli."

Charli put down her plate, remembering some of Uncle Will's other surprises. He taught history at Mount Pleasant High, and one summer, the day after school closed, he'd bought a secondhand boat, "guaranteed to give us all a perfect vacation." The boat had sunk like a rock with the whole family on board. Even though it was moored in shallow water when it went down, the shock had been terrible. The next summer he'd invited the family to come out to Eagle Hill to watch his first hang-gliding lesson. He'd broken his leg when he landed.

The worst surprise—Charli groaned, remembering—was the summer he'd painted the Bellands' house the incredibly bright blue it was now, while Charli and her mother were away on a camping trip.

"I wanted to surprise you," he told them proudly, when they returned. "Turned out a little brighter than I expected, but you'll get used to it."

"What kind of surprise is it, Dad?" Dan broke the silence. "Give us a clue."

"No can do," Uncle Will said gleefully. "You

might just try to talk me out of it." He scooped up a ball lying at the foot of the steps and jumped to his feet. "Catch!" he bellowed, tossing it toward the twins. He dived to retrieve it as it came bouncing back.

Charli looked at Dan, speechless.

"Oh, quit worrying," her cousin muttered. "A month from now he'll probably have forgotten all about the surprise, whatever it is."

The screen door flapped behind them, and Charli looked over her shoulder to see her brand-new stepfather. He was watching Uncle Will, who shouted and pretended to tackle first one twin, then the other. Ray winked at Charli and went back into the kitchen, but not before she'd seen his expression. He had been eyeing Uncle Will as if he were an alien from another planet.

"Ray thinks we're not his kind of people," she muttered. "He thinks we're strange."

"Well, we're not," Dan retorted. "Ray's been around here long enough to know what our family is like. Besides, if Dad's going to do something weird again, it won't affect you. That's *our* problem."

"Ours, too. We're all one family," Charli said stubbornly. She looked up at the sky, half-expecting to see a black trouble-cloud sail over the house. "Uncle Will mentioned my mom," she reminded Dan. "So we're mixed up in the surprise, and that means Ray will be, too. He won't like it."

She already knew what her stepfather thought of at least one of Uncle Will's surprises. The day before the wedding he had mentioned that he hoped there would be time to paint the house a sensible color before school started this fall.

Chapter Two

SOPHIA'S JOURNAL

I should have given you a name a long time ago. After all, you've been my best friend ever since I moved in with my great-grandmother. It wasn't only that she never talked; it was as if she lived in this circle of quiet and no one else existed. I started writing to you that very first night.

Right now I imagine you sitting up in bed, same as I am, only you're in your own room in your own house, and you know everyone else who lives there and you love them all. You might even be wearing a Save the Animals T-shirt like mine—not that it matters. The important thing is, you listen. I can tell you stuff, like why I'm not in my great-grandmother's apartment anymore, and why I don't expect to be in this place long either.

I'll start with the cab ride in Madison this morning, because that's when I knew for sure my life was about to change again. It was my first ride in a cab, and I bet it was the first for my great-grandmother, too. Not that she said so, of course. All the way to the hospital she stared out the window, her wrinkled face as still as stone.

When I first met her, a year and a half ago, her face was pink and puckered. Now the puckers are like deep cuts carved into gray skin. I know she's going to die soon. I bet she knows it, too. I want to feel bad, because after all she's the only relative I have left, but I can't. Sorry about that. She's as much a stranger today as she was when I moved in.

We were pulling up in front of St. Joseph's Hospital when she finally spoke. "Your great-grandfather had a niece in Mount Pleasant. Nice girl. Maybe you can stay with her for a while."

Naturally I had about a million questions I wanted to ask, but I just said okay because she wasn't going to tell me anything else. It was as if she'd peered out for a moment from that weird, silent place where she lives, and she'd noticed me next to her, and she'd said what she had to say. Period.

I was beginning to feel pretty weird myself. I knew the feeling because I've had it before, quite a few times. One minute I'm safe—well, semi-safe—and the next I'm floating in space. If I was an astronaut, that would be the moment when the line that attached me to my ship slipped away. Suddenly there's no up, no down, no *connections*. That's exactly how I felt then, sitting in the cab with my poor dying great-grandmother.

When you lose your connection, everything seems far away. A pointy-faced doctor examined my great-grandmother in the emergency room and scolded her for waiting so long to come to the hospital. After he left there were two nurses, a young one with red hair who smiled a lot and an older one who told me to follow her down a hall.

"I understand your grandmother is your guardian," she said. "Our social worker will help you sort things out. She's very efficient."

Whenever I hear "social worker" I start to worry. This one—her name tag said Rita—was nice enough, but she asked the same old questions other social workers had asked a hundred times.

"Your great-grandmother is very sick," she said, finally. "We'll try to help her, but you'll need someplace to stay until she gets better. I can make some arrangements, or you can go back to—where was it, Sacramento?"

I told her about the niece in Mount Pleasant,

but she looked doubtful. "We'll talk to your great-grandmother," she said, and I thought, Lots of luck!

We went back down the hall to the same elevator that had taken my great-grandmother away. When we stepped out onto the seventh floor, the smell of disinfectant made me want to throw up. I glanced into some rooms, but the faces that looked back at me were so sad that I turned away fast.

My great-grandmother was in a room by herself, lying on a high narrow bed. Her eyes were closed, and her bony little hands were folded on the tan blanket. Her eyes flicked open when we came in.

I stood near the door and waited while Rita asked questions about the niece in Mount Pleasant. I couldn't hear her answers, but I don't think she knew much to tell. Suddenly her eyes snapped shut again, and she began to snore.

Rita stood looking at her as if she wasn't sure what to do next. "Do you want to kiss her good-bye?" she asked.

I said I didn't think so. We had never kissed.

As we walked back to the elevator, Rita kept sighing and reading her notes. "I suppose this will be okay," she said doubtfully. "Your great-grandmother's your guardian, after all. If this woman in Mount Pleasant is willing . . ." She sighed some more and then seemed to make up her mind. "Well, it's a good thing school's out, isn't it?" she said in a chirpy voice. "This can be like a vacation for you, Sophia. You can write to your great-grandmother and tell her your adventures."

I groaned, not out loud. She had no idea how crazy that was. My great-grandmother hadn't even known I existed until the Social Services people in Sacramento called her. They had just discovered there was a member of the Weyer family still alive in Madison, Wisconsin. They told her about me, how I'd been in a whole string of foster homes, and wouldn't she just love to have me come to Madison?

I was pretty excited, finding I actually had a relative, but the whole thing was a mistake. My great-grandmother should have said no when she had the chance. I guess it didn't matter to her whether I came or not. She was like a sleepwalker, cleaning her apartment, cooking rice with canned vegetables, crocheting shawls that were never used. When I came home from school each afternoon, she always seemed a little surprised, as if she'd forgotten I lived with her.

Rita waited for me to say something chirpy-cheery back at her, but I couldn't think of a thing. "My great-grandma can't read English," I told her finally. "Anyway, she's going to die. She won't expect a letter."

There it was, the first mistake of the day. Rita's face turned pink, and she walked faster. Back in her office, she got Lilly Crandall's telephone number from information, and sure enough, Lilly Crandall was okay with my coming, just the way my great-grandmother had been a year and a half ago. I wondered if Lilly would turn out to be another sleepwalker.

We drove to my great-grandmother's apartment on Johnson Avenue, and Rita cleaned out the refrigerator while I packed my things. I put jeans and tops and underwear and socks in one suitcase, and my books and CD's in the other. I hadn't played the CD's since I left Sacramento, but I didn't want to leave them behind.

When I came out of the bedroom, Rita was at the kitchen window. She looked worried.

"We're moving pretty fast on this, Sophia," she said. "Isn't there someone in Madison you want to call to tell them where you'll be?"

"There's nobody," I said. "When I moved here, a caseworker came for a while, but she hasn't been around for a long time. My great-grandmother told her to mind her own business."

"What about your friends at school?"

I just shrugged. When you worry all the time about saying the wrong thing, it's hard to make friends.

Rita rolled her eyes and sighed again. "Okay, okay," she said. "Anyway, Mrs. Crandall sounds very pleasant, and I guess you can take care of yourself. Meeting new people is fun if you have the right attitude."

I could tell she didn't think I had it.

I wondered about that while she drove us to the bus station. Jim and Judy Stengel were my first foster parents after my mom died. Maybe I did have the right attitude then, because I stayed with them for three years. Then, when I was ten, I knew—all of a sudden—that they were going to go away and leave me. The day Jim finally said he'd been transferred to London, I wasn't even surprised. Judy hugged me and cried when I told her I'd known, but she didn't believe me.

"You must have overheard us talking about it," she said.

That was when I understood I was different from other kids. It wasn't only that I sometimes knew things before they happened, though that was a big part of it. I wasn't good enough or nice enough or *something* enough to be part of a family. If I had been, the Stengels would have found a way to take me to London with them.

For a while I moved from one foster home to another—some okay, one very bad. What I tried to do mostly was be invisible. I felt safer if I could make people forget I was around.

Then I went to live with the Wagners. They were really nice, like the Stengels, and they said their daughter Linda needed a sister. I liked that, even though Linda told me the first day that she didn't want a sister. I was sure I could find ways to make her glad I was there.

By that time I was getting used to knowing things before they happened. Some times it was just a feeling—like a hunch—and other times a picture of what was coming popped into my head as clear as anything. Either way, you can bet I didn't tell the Wagners when it happened. I hoped that if I ignored it, after a while the whole weird thing would go away.

That worked until the day Linda got suspended for cheating on a math test. She said I must have told Mrs. Holmgren. The reason she said so was because the day before the test I mentioned to her that kids who cheated were going to get in trouble. I thought it was all right to say that much—being her sister—but I was wrong.

A couple of weeks later I was standing in front of my school locker when a really scary thing happened. The hall went dark and the walls just seemed to fall away. The darkness only lasted a second or two, but it was enough. That afternoon I took home everything I cared about—the snapshot of my mom and dad, my old blue sweatshirt, the folder of stories I wrote for English class. Some other stuff.

I said I had a headache that evening and stayed in my bedroom, which was okay with the Wagners. I kept hoping I was wrong this time, but about ten-thirty sirens started screaming. Cars raced by and people yelled. The Wagners ran outside to see what had happened, but I stayed where I was. I knew.

When I went downstairs the next morning, Linda was practically jumping up and down with excitement.

"You knew!" she said, sounding so happy. "Sophia knew, Dad! Maybe she didn't set the fire herself, but she knew someone was going to do it. She cleaned out her locker yesterday!"

Mrs. Wagner said, "Don't be silly, Linda. That's a terrible thing to say." She smacked her coffee cup down on its saucer hard enough to spill.

Mr. Wagner was real quiet for a moment, and then he said, "*Did* you bring your things home, Sophia?"

I said yes, I had just felt like doing that. No special reason.

It sounded like a lie, even to me. He looked at me and at Linda, and then at me again, as if he was beginning to see lots of problems ahead. Having his daughter suspended for cheating had been bad enough; now he might have a firebug on his hands. A big-time troublemaker! I could tell exactly what he was thinking, and I was pretty sure right then that I wouldn't be living with the Wagners much longer.

"Here we are," Rita said, turning into a parking lot next to the bus station. "Just in time, too. If my watch is right, the bus to Mount Pleasant is due to leave in seven minutes."

I came back to the present with a jolt. Bus station? Mount Pleasant? I didn't even know what she was talking about. I must have looked dazed, because she patted my shoulder.

"I think your bus is that one over there," she said, pointing. "You take the suitcases and stand in line, and I'll run inside and buy your ticket."

I nodded and smiled at her, but my heart wasn't in it. Whenever I think about the Stengels and the Wagners and all the places where I've been in between, I feel as if I'm out there in space again, with nothing to hold on to. I'd sort of forgotten about that space thing while I lived with my great-grandmother, but now it was back.

I saw Rita come out of the station and push through the crowds that were gathering around the buses. She looked tired, and I knew she didn't want to be there—for other reasons, besides the fact that she still wasn't sure sending me to Mount Pleasant was the right thing to do.

"Look," I said when she handed me the ticket, "you can go home now if you want to. I'll be okay. Thanks for helping."

The line moved forward, but she still stood there, biting her lip. "Thanks again," I said, and then, wouldn't you know, the rest just came tumbling out. "You'd better go, or you'll miss your phone call."

The line moved again, and I stepped up into the bus. I heard Rita gasp behind me as I handed my ticket to the driver. I pushed past people to a seat in the very back of the bus. Crouched as far down as I could get, I called myself every name I could think of. Stupid! Big mouth! What if she followed me on the bus and demanded to know what I'd meant about that phone call?

I didn't mean anything, Rita, I'd say. It was a mistake. I make mistakes like that sometimes.

It seemed forever before the doors closed with a shuddering sigh. Then the bus growled and jerked forward, out of the terminal and into the late afternoon sunlight.

I sat up and looked out the window. We chugged through downtown Madison, gradually picking up speed until we were out on the highway. You can bet I was tired and scared, but most of all I was mad at myself. Maybe Rita was calling Lilly Crandall right then to tell her Sophia Weyer was a weirdo. I was pretty sure she wouldn't do that, but if she did I wouldn't blame her.

KEEP YOUR MOUTH SHUT! I told myself. That's my Rule Number One, and if I can't remember it, I'm going to be floating out there in space the rest of my life.

Chapter Three
CHARLI

When the cake was eaten and the paper plates gathered up, the Crandalls went home, trailing noise and laughter behind them. Ray stayed. Well, sure, Charli reminded herself, he lives here now. Still, it felt strange. At five in the afternoon most days her mother would be at the restaurant putting in overtime, but today she and Ray were out in the kitchen, talking. Her mother sounded younger than usual, Charli thought, her voice sort of breathy, even girlish. The cheerleaders at school sounded like that—as if the world were so exciting they could hardly stand it.

She looked around the living room. Ray had started moving his things into the house a week ago, so she was already accustomed to the pile of *Sports Illustrated* magazines on the coffee table and the sturdy green recliner that he said he couldn't leave behind. It was a clunky old chair, with worn spots on the cushions and coffee stains on the armrests, but Charli's mother hadn't said a word.

Charli threw herself into the chair and tugged at the scarred wooden lever that made the back tilt. The lever squeaked, and the voices in the kitchen stopped.

"Is that you, hon?"

Charli sat very still, breathing the good smell of the chair and waiting. Her mother and Ray came in from the kitchen.

"I thought you went across the street with Dan," her mother said. "Why are you sitting in here all by yourself?"

"No reason," Charli said. "This chair squeaks."

"I know," Ray said apologetically. "I guess I've just gotten used to it."

"And there's lots of spots on the arms."

"Charli!" her mother said. "For goodness' sake!" She sounded annoyed, but Ray laughed. "I've gotten used to those, too," he said. "Good thing your mom says she knows how to get rid of them. Not tonight, though. Right now we have other things to do—like getting ready for the homecoming dinner."

Charli pulled her feet up under her and sank deeper into the chair. Nobody had told her about a homecoming dinner.

"We're going to drive into Racine for dinner," her mother said cheerfully. "At a restaurant that overlooks Lake Michigan. Doesn't that sound great?"

"All of us?" Charli uncoiled her legs and sat up.

"Well, of course, you, too," her mother said.

"Does Aunt Lilly know?" Charli asked. "She'll think the twins and Mickey are too little to go."

"And she'd be right," Ray said. "This is just for us, Charli. The three of us. Our first dinner as a family."

Charli pulled the lever hard, and the old chair catapulted her onto her feet. Her mother and Ray burst out laughing. "Our first dinner as a family . . . she likes the way that sounds as much as I do," her mother said. "Change into something besides shorts, Charli. This is special."

Charli nodded and ran down the hall to her bedroom. Her face was hot and her stomach was too full of wedding cake, but she hardly noticed. She pulled her blue pants and the matching top from a dresser drawer. Then she hurried to the bathroom and splashed cold water on her face until she gasped for breath. As she buried her face in a towel she could almost hear Dan laughing at her.

"What's the big deal?" he'd want to know. "Ray's had dinner with you and your mom lots of times."

That was true, but as Charli put on the blue outfit and brushed her damp hair, she felt a surge of relief. Ray had said the words himself: *Our first dinner as a family.* He was reminding her that he hadn't just married her mom, he'd married her kid, too. She stared at herself in the mirror over her dresser and straightened her glasses.

Through the open window she could hear Ray out in the driveway, emptying the last of the luggage from the car so there would be room for three people to ride. She tiptoed down the hall, past the open door to her mother's bedroom and back to the living room. Across the street the Crandalls' house was quiet.

"Let's go," she called to her mother. "Let's go right now."

"Oh, Charli," her mother called back, "calm down. The restaurant will wait for us."

Charli kept her eyes on the house across the street while Ray backed the car out of the driveway and she and her mother climbed in. There was only one thing that could spoil this moment and it didn't happen. Not a single Crandall appeared to see them leave. Charli was glad. She didn't want Uncle Will and Aunt Lilly and the cousins to know they weren't invited to the family dinner.

Three hours later, a taxi made a U-turn and stopped in front of the Crandalls' house just as Charli and her parents turned onto Lincoln Street.

"The new kid!" Charli exclaimed. In the excitement of the beautiful restaurant, the lake with the yachts skimming by, the cloth napkins as big as hand towels, too many forks, too much chicken and not enough shrimp, and the perfect slice of chocolate peanut butter pie, she had forgotten about the girl who was coming to live with the Crandalls. Now she watched curiously as a dark figure stepped out of the cab, dragging a big suitcase and then a smaller one behind her.

The girl stood uncertainly at the curb until the

taxi pulled away. Then she started up the walk, wobbling a little under the weight of her bags.

"Poor child," Charli's mother said. "Lilly didn't know whether she was coming tonight or tomorrow. She was supposed to call as soon as she got in, so they could pick her up downtown."

Ray swung into the driveway just as the Crandalls' front door opened and Aunt Lilly came out onto the porch. Charli unfastened her seatbelt and opened the car door before Ray turned off the motor.

"I'm going over there," she said excitedly. "I want to see what she's like."

"Oh, Charli," her mother protested. "It's so late. Why don't you wait until morning? The girl must be tired and you're tired—"

"I'm not tired," Charli said.

She was halfway back to the street when Ray said, "Hey!" in a way that made her skid to a stop. "Think about what it must be like to come to a strange house all by yourself, not knowing anybody, Charli. She doesn't need another stranger staring at her, checking out whether she's pretty and fun." His voice softened. "Your mother's right. There'll be plenty of time tomorrow to get to know her."

Charli's cheeks burned. He was *bossing* her!

And how had he guessed exactly what she'd wanted to find out? Slowly she walked back down the driveway and followed the grown-ups into the house. I was just going to say hi, she thought angrily. The new girl couldn't be too tired for that.

Later, when she was in bed, she heard Ray's low voice and then her mother's down the hall.

"—don't see why Will and Lilly would do it," Ray said. "They have more kids than they can handle without taking on another one."

"It'll work out," Charli's mother said. "Will may be a little impulsive and Lilly may be a little disorganized but—"

"A little?" Ray chuckled. "A little! I feel sorry for the new arrival. She has a lot to get used to over there."

Charli punched her pillow and dived farther under the sheet, covering her ears. It was just what she'd dreaded—Ray didn't understand the Crandalls at all.

I don't feel one bit sorry for the new girl, she thought furiously. Anyone who lives with Uncle Will and Aunt Lilly is lucky!

Chapter Four

SOPHIA'S JOURNAL

Tonight when I stepped off the bus in Mount Pleasant, I felt as if I was landing on the moon. I wished I could stay on the bus, if you can believe that.

"Over there," the driver called after me. He pointed across the street. "That's the only cab in town, and you'd better grab it. This is his last stop before he goes home."

I had a telephone number I was supposed to call, but I carried my suitcases over to the cab instead. I guess I wanted to put off meeting Lilly Crandall as long as possible. When I gave the old driver the address, he said, "Yup, the Crandalls," and grinned. I wondered if he knew the address of everyone in town.

The Crandalls' house is old, with a wide front porch big enough for chairs and a swing. A tall blond woman in jeans and a man's shirt opened the screen door almost the moment I knocked.

"Oh, Sophia, for goodness' sake!" she said, as if we'd known each other forever. "Why didn't you call when you got in? We would have come to pick you up. Well, never mind, you're here now, and that's all that matters. I'm Lilly Crandall and this is our son Dan."

"Hi," the boy said. He's tall and thin, and he sort of *unfolded* from the couch where he'd been lying with his head on a paunchy gorilla's stomach. Lilly swept some blocks off a chair so I could sit down.

I never saw a room as messy as that one. I don't mean it was dirty, just a mess. There were toy trucks and cars everywhere, and parts of puzzles and some torn coloring books. Broken crayons were scattered across the carpet.

I started to say "Thanks for letting me come," but Lilly was talking again a mile a minute.

"We've got a bed ready for you in the catchall room upstairs, Sophia. It's kind of cluttered now, but we'll clean it out, and then you can fix it up the way you like it. Our baby Mickey has been sleeping in there, but I've moved him into the twins' room.

You'll meet them tomorrow—after you've had a good night's sleep." She chuckled as if a good night's sleep was important before meeting the twins.

I said, quickly, before she started talking again, "Thanks for saying it was all right for me to come." It sounded stiff and standoffish, but it was the best I could do.

Lilly said, "Well, of course it's all right. Your great-grandpa was one of my favorite people when I was a little girl. I miss him! I never did get to know your great-grandma very well, but I'm glad she remembered me."

I sat still and let her words flow around me. They warmed up that numb place inside of me.

"I'll take your stuff upstairs," Dan offered. But before he could move, a tall gray-haired man appeared, clutching a cardboard box stacked high with papers. When he saw me, he set the box on the floor and hurried across the room to shake hands. "Welcome aboard, Susie."

Lilly said, "It's not Susie. Sophia Weyer, this is my husband, Will. He's the one who makes things happen around here." When she said that, the overflowing stack of papers in the box slid sideways and spread across the floor, adding to the mess.

"That's my filing system, Su-Sophia," Will said.

He gathered the papers into a pile and dropped them on top of the other papers that remained in the box. By the time he stood up again, his hair was standing up straight and his horn-rimmed glasses were at an angle on his nose.

"Don't look so concerned, Sophia," he said. "Lilly and Dan will tell you, we don't let little things bother us in this family."

"Will teaches history at the high school," Lilly told me proudly. "You might have him for a teacher this fall."

"I doubt it," Will said. "How old are you, Sophia?"

I said, "Fourteen."

"Well, then, no," he said. "I teach juniors and seniors, and by the time you're that old . . ."

What was he going to say? By the time I'm a junior I won't be living in Mount Pleasant? Probably. It doesn't really matter, because the moment I saw him I wanted to run out the door and never come back.

Will Crandall means trouble. Don't ask me how I know, I just do. I know it, as sure as I know his glasses were on crooked and he needs a haircut. He's a dangerous person, not cruel or wicked, but dangerous just the same.

I felt as if I should warn somebody right then, maybe warn *him*, but of course I didn't. I just stood there looking stupid and wondering where I can go when the Crandalls find out how weird I am. Where else is there?

Chapter Five

CHARLI

"What's she like?" Charli demanded. She had rushed through breakfast so she could be outside when Dan left for his shift at The Best Yet Burger. Now she was running to keep up with his long strides. His expression, closed off and grim, was so different from his usual look that she guessed the new girl must be awful.

"Tell me," she repeated. "I won't tell anyone what you say. I just want to know."

Dan walked faster. "She's okay," he said gruffly. "Her name is Sophia Weyer and she doesn't talk much. She went to bed almost as soon as she got here. That's all."

"No, it isn't," Charli insisted. "I can tell by your face. Something's wrong!"

They had reached the corner when, unexpectedly, Dan stopped. "Okay, so something's wrong," he admitted. "You'll hear about it soon enough. My dad's heading to your house as soon as he finishes breakfast. And believe me, it has nothing to do with Sophia the Silent." With that, he strode off down the street.

"What's 'it'?" she called after him forlornly, but he didn't answer.

When she turned back, Uncle Will and Aunt Lilly were climbing the front steps of her house. Without the kids, Charli marveled. That was odd. Aunt Lilly never went anywhere without the twins and Mickey if Dan wasn't there to look after them. Sophia Weyer must be the baby-sitter this morning. She walked faster at the thought that whatever the Crandalls wanted to talk about was important enough to make them leave the children with an almost-stranger.

"You're just in time, Charli!" Uncle Will called from the kitchen when she opened the front door. "You know, I told you yesterday I couldn't talk about my big surprise for a while? Well, I got it all straightened out in my head last night and set up the paperwork. We're ready to go." He smiled at Aunt Lilly, who smiled back. "I told the boys about it at breakfast this morning."

Charli pulled the tall kitchen stool up to the table and helped herself to a doughnut.

"I've just made the biggest decision of my life," Uncle Will said grandly. "*Our* lives. You know the new water park that's going to be built on the lake road next year?"

Charli nodded. Everyone in Mount Pleasant had heard about the water park.

"Well, there's going to be a lot of people coming to town for vacations once that's built," Uncle Will went on. "And they're going to need rooms to stay in. That's where we come in. I'm grabbing the one perfect place in town to fix up for a bed-and-breakfast. It's beautiful and it's close to where the park will be, and we're going to make a fortune with it!"

"A bed-and-breakfast?" Charli's mother repeated. "You, Will?"

"All of us." Uncle Will waved his arms. "I know Lilly has too much to do at home to be the housekeeper, but she'll be able to help out once in a while, and we can always hire a couple of women from town to do the cleaning. What I was hoping, Rona," he said to Charli's mother, "is that you'll be our hostess and cook. You'd like that—never having to wait on tables at the diner again. Am I right?" He leaned back, smiling expectantly.

They stared at him. "Where is this 'perfect place,' Will?" Ray asked slowly. "I know where the park's going to be, but I can't think of any house near it that could possibly become a bed-and-breakfast."

"Yes, you can!" Uncle Will insisted. "Sure you can! You can see it from our backyard—about two blocks away as the crow flies."

"*I* know," Charli's mom said, looking at Aunt Lilly. "It's that place they call the Castle."

Charli knew it, too. "But it's haunted!" she exclaimed. "Everybody says it's haunted."

"Haunted by rats and termites," Ray said sharply. "You're not serious, Will. You can't be talking about buying that old wreck."

"Sure am," Uncle Will said. "It's not a wreck, folks, it's a beautiful *mansion*. All it needs is a little fixing up—well, a lot of fixing up. And, Charli, if it's haunted, so much the better. There's people who'd pay good money to sleep in a gen-uine haunted house."

Ray fired more questions at Uncle Will, but Charli hardly heard the answers. The Castle! She had walked past it a hundred times, always with a little shiver of excitement. It just had to be haunted! Once she'd even tried the locked front door, though she never would have gone inside alone. Now Uncle Will was going to own it, and he would probably be there most of the time, so she could go in whenever she wanted.

Her thoughts flew, imagining what it would be like. She might discover a real ghost and get her picture in the paper. Every kid in school would want to get inside to look around, but they would have to ask her first. It was her uncle's house, so she would decide who could come in and who couldn't.

"What do *you* think, Lilly?" Ray demanded suddenly. "You're not going along with this, are you?"

Aunt Lilly laid a hand on Uncle Will's arm. "I want what Will wants," she said. "If he says it'll work, I'm sure he's right."

"Ray just means we hope it's a wise thing to do, Will," Charli's mother said anxiously. "It would be terrible to take money out of your savings and then lose it."

"But I won't lose it," Uncle Will told them confidently. "You'll see, Rona. This will be the best move I've ever made. I know the place looks pretty bad now, but I'm going to spend the summer fixing it up. Before you know it, people will be banging at the door, wanting to invest. Then there'll be enough money to furnish the house in style." He turned to Charli and said, "What do *you* think, young lady?"

"I think it's great," Charli said, careful not to look at Ray. "I'll help you find out about the ghost. I love ghost stories!"

Everyone laughed at that except Ray.

"I can use your help, Charli," Uncle Will assured her. "The pay won't be much, but I'll make it up to you late when the money starts rolling in."

"Oh, you don't have to pay me," Charli said. "Maybe the new girl can help, too."

"The new girl," Uncle Will repeated, as if he'd already forgotten there was a new girl. "Oh, yes—Sophia. Sure, she might be glad to have a job. I'll talk to her about it."

"I wanted to come over last night," Charli said with a reproachful sigh, "but—I couldn't. I wanted to say hello because I thought she'd be kind of scared, coming to a strange place all by herself. I wanted to make her feel better."

Her mother groaned. "Don't be such a drama queen, Charli," she scolded. "Ray was right and you know it."

"Sophia's settling in just fine, dear," Aunt Lilly said. "She was awfully tired last night and went to bed right away, but we'll all get to know one another today. You come over whenever you want."

Charli looked quickly at Ray. That's how things are in this family, she wanted to tell him. We go back and forth across the street whenever we want to. But Ray clearly hadn't been listening. He was leaning back in his chair and looking at Uncle Will, his lips pursed tightly as if he could just barely suppress an ocean-sized flood of disapproval.

Chapter Six

SOPHIA'S JOURNAL

What's worse than two tornadoes? This is no joke, so don't try to figure out the punch line. The answer is, Four-year-old twins. I've moved around a lot, and I thought I was ready for anything, but Gene and Terry Crandall are something special. Or else it just seems that way after the quiet of my great-grandmother's apartment.

I woke up to giggling, and for a moment I didn't know where I was. Then I saw my suitcases and I remembered everything that had happened yesterday. While I was sorting it out, the door opened slowly, and a small blond head appeared, then another. They must have been shoving each other, because suddenly both kids tumbled into the room. When I sat up and said hi, they scrambled to their feet and backed out, still giggling. They sounded like a whole herd of horses on the uncarpeted stairs.

I dressed in a hurry and brushed my hair, standing at the window while I braided it again. This room looks out on a street of pleasant old houses, all pretty much the same except for the bright blue one across the street. There's a stop sign at one end of the block, and the other end changes to gravel and curves into open fields. Lincoln Street must be on the edge of town.

While I stood there the front door banged, and Dan Crandall came out. He walked fast with his shoulders sort of hunched, as if he was in a big hurry to get away.

The twin tornadoes were pelting each other with Cheerios when I got to the kitchen, but the grown-ups ignored them. Will was studying some papers next to his coffee cup, and Lilly sat with their baby on her lap. Will looked rumpled and Lilly looked contented, which, I think now, is the way they pretty much are *all* the time.

Will said good morning and so did I, and then he went right back to his papers. I was glad, because I didn't want to talk to him—I couldn't. Lilly chattered a mile a minute while I ate toast and drank orange juice.

"Your baby's beautiful," I said when she stopped

for breath, and her face glowed. I'm sure lots of people have told her that, because he really is beautiful. His name is Michael, or Mickey, in honor of Will's father, but he has Lilly's blue eyes and blond hair. He smiled across the table at me every minute or so, and then went back to watching the twins as if they were putting on a great show just for him.

When I finished my toast, Lilly came around the table and put Mickey on my lap. "He takes to some people quicker than others," she said. What I love about babies is that you don't have to pretend with them. They don't care if you're weird, as long as they think you mean well, which I do. I mean well.

Holding Mickey was the nicest thing that had happened to me in a long time. It felt so good that I said sure when Lilly asked if I'd mind taking care of him for a few minutes. She and Will had to go across the street to talk to Will's sister Rona. We could sit out in the backyard, she said, and the twins could play in the sandbox.

I realized then that Gene and Terry were part of the baby-sitting package. They must have been as surprised as I was, because the Cheerios stopped flying and they stared as if they were seeing me for the first time.

It wasn't too bad at first. Lilly went out to the

sandbox with us and got the twins settled, digging a hole for a lake.

I sat across from them and helped Mickey spoon sand into a pail. The yard is the kind I like—beds of bright flowers, and toys scattered everywhere. Birds sang in the trees at the end of the yard, and Mickey made little chuckly sounds every time he managed to get a few grains of sand into the pail. Gene and Terry poured water from a sprinkling can into their lake.

And then the peace ended. "The water won't stay!" Gene yelled, as if it was his brother's fault. "I'll get the hose."

He started for the side of the house, but I jumped up, clutching Mickey under one arm and grabbing for Gene with the other. "The hose won't help," I said. "Sand won't hold water."

He yelled, "It will, too!" and pulled so hard that I almost stumbled over a battered blue plastic dishpan lying in the grass. I let go of Gene and handed the dishpan to Terry.

"Use that for a lake," I told him. "Then the water won't leak out."

"Want the hose!" Gene yelled louder than ever, but he came back to the sandbox. Soon both boys were digging to make the pan fit.

I wished the Crandalls would finish up their business across the street in a hurry.

"Make some hills around the lake," I suggested.

"Don't want hills," Gene said. "We need an island." He scooped up two handfuls of sand and dropped them into the dishpan, turning the water to mud. Terry roared and hit him, Mickey started to scream, and Gene threw more sand into the water.

I felt like screaming, too, but I said, "Hey, that's a swamp. I bet it's full of snakes and alligators."

The twins stared into the dishpan.

"And crocodiles!" Gene said with a really blood-thirsty grin. He picked up a toy soldier and plunged it into the mud.

"That was pretty smart," a voice said behind me. "I never know what to do when they all start yelling at once."

A girl stood there watching me, her eyes full of questions behind dark-rimmed glasses. She said, "My name is Charli Belland. I live across the street—I'm the cousin."

I said hi and told her my name, which I could tell she already knew.

"Charli has a new dad," Gene said, still staring into the swamp. "Now she has a mom and dad like everybody else."

I said, "That's nice. You're lucky."

Charli's face got pink. "I guess," she said, talking fast. "Ray's okay even if he's sort of bossy. I wanted to come over to meet you last night, and my mother would have let me, but he said no. He said you had enough to get used to without me hanging around. Well, he didn't say those words, but it's what he meant."

She waited for me to say I wish she'd come, but I was thinking that this Ray must be a nice guy.

"I was pretty tired," I told her. "I went to bed right away."

"Well, Aunt Lilly and Uncle Will are *very* easy to get used to," she went on, as if she was settling an argument. "And so is Dan. He's sort of like my big brother. The little kids get wild sometimes, but you won't have to take care of them much when we start working."

I interrupted before she could race on to another subject. "Working? Where?"

She looked surprised. "At the Castle. Didn't Uncle Will tell you about the Castle this morning? He just told my mom and Ray and me. Dan is really mad about it, but I'm not. I think it's great. We'll have fun."

I must have looked as mixed up as I felt, because she took a deep breath and started over. "The

Castle's a big old house on Barker Street. Uncle Will is buying it for a bed-and-breakfast place." She pointed toward the tangle of trees and underbrush at the end of the yard. "Go through that little woods and look across the field, and you can see it yourself. Everybody says it's haunted, and when we work there we can find out for sure. We can be ghostbusters."

"No way!" I said, so sharply that the twins stopped tossing their little toy trucks in the swamp and Mickey looked up at me in surprise.

All kinds of alarms were going off in my head. Was this why Lilly and Will had invited me to stay with them? So I could work for them?

"What's wrong?" Charli asked. "Don't you want to help Uncle Will? It would just be for a couple of hours every day."

"I don't know anything about a job," I told her. "I just got here, remember. And I don't believe in ghosts. That's childish."

She looked as if I'd slapped her. Writing all this down, I can see how cranky I sounded. I didn't want to be like that, but I wanted her to stop talking. I didn't want to be a ghostbuster—I just wanted all of them to stop pretending to be my friend so I would do what they wanted me to do.

"There are too ghosts," Charli said. "I have a whole book about ghosts right here in Wisconsin."

Gene said, "Hey, are you guys fighting?"

I told him no, but when I looked back at Charli I saw that we were. Well, I didn't care. She has everything—a mother and a father and a home of her own. She's probably lived on this street all her life, and she's never had to worry about a thing. She made me sick.

"I probably won't be here very long, anyway," I told her. "As soon as my great-grandmother gets better, I'll go back to Madison."

It was a big relief when Lilly came around the side of the house. The twins raced to meet her and dragged her over to the sandbox so she could admire their swamp.

She said, "How nice that you girls are getting to know each other. You'll have lots of good times this summer." Then she said she was taking the three boys to town to buy shoes and we could come along if we wanted to.

Charli said, "I have to go home. I have stuff to do." She hurried away without saying good-bye to anyone. I said I'd stay home, if that was okay with her.

"Of course, it's okay," she said. "You do whatever you want to. Will's inside if you need anything." She gathered up the boys and hustled them off into the house to wash the mud off their hands and faces and knees.

When they were gone I closed my eyes and took deep breaths. I did that a lot at my great-grandmother's place. And I did it a lot those last weeks with the Wagners, when I knew they wanted me to leave but didn't come right out and say it. Just breathe and stare at the inside of your eyelids and wait, until you don't care anymore.

After a while I went down to the end of the yard. It wasn't a real woods back there, just a band of trees and brush that extended across all the backyards on this side of the street. Someone had worn a narrow path through it and into a wide field of grass and thistles and wildflowers. There was a row of small houses on the other side of the field, and beyond them I could see a tall, peaked roof like a witch's hat. Stretches of roof extended out on either side of it, and chimneys poked up here and there. The Castle.

It was funny looking, a joke of a house, but it made me uneasy just the same. If the Crandalls let me come to Mount Pleasant so I could work there, they made a mistake. I'm not going to do it, and nobody can make me. Not Will Crandall and not Lilly, and definitely not that spoiled kid from across the street.

Chapter Seven

CHARLI

Charli could hardly believe how much life had changed in the last few days. For one thing, her house seemed so *crowded*. Ray had come to dinner many times in the weeks and months before the wedding, and he had cut the grass and helped with other chores, but now he lived there. He and her mother talked and laughed until late at night, and the sound of his footsteps in the hall woke Charli each morning. By the time she got up, he had made coffee and poured orange juice and set the cereal boxes in a row on the table. *Just as if he belongs here,* she'd thought each morning, and then had to remind herself, *He does, stupid!*

Why was that so hard to get used to? And

why did she feel as if Ray were constantly criticizing the way she looked and judging what she said? He wasn't like that. He wasn't mean. Yet whenever he teased her about watching too much television or eating too much ice cream, she felt hurt.

Once, she would have gone across the street to talk to Aunt Lilly about it, but not now. That part of her life had changed, too. Sophia Weyer was living in the Crandalls' house now, helping Aunt Lilly in the kitchen or playing with the little boys. Charli couldn't talk to Aunt Lilly about Ray with Sophia there listening, deciding what was childish and what wasn't.

"There must be something you can do to keep yourself busy," Ray had said this morning. "Call up a friend, Charli. Go for a bike ride."

There was no one, Charli had told him, feeling more pitiful by the minute. Her best friend, Heather, was at camp, and her second-best friend, Carissa, was spending the summer with her grandmother in Green Bay.

"Then why not go over and help your aunt?" he suggested, sounding impatient. "Goodness knows she can use it."

"She doesn't need me. She has Sophia," Charli mumbled and was immediately sorry.

Ray sighed, picked up the newspaper, and ignored her until Rona was ready for work. Then they went off together, and Charli was left to spend another morning reading under the crab apple tree in the backyard until she fell asleep.

"Man, some people are lucky!" The voice was so close that she woke with a little scream. "What a life!" Dan said. "It must be great to lie around while everyone else is slaving."

Charli scowled up at her cousin. He smelled like hamburgers even before he went to work, and today there were tight little worry lines in his forehead.

"I'm going to have a job pretty soon, too," she retorted. "Uncle Will wants me to help him fix up the Castle. I'm resting so I'll be ready."

Dan leaned against the tree trunk. "And what do you think you're going to do there?" he asked sarcastically. "Put on a new roof? Paint all the window frames?"

Charli hesitated. She didn't know what Uncle Will expected her to do. "There'll be lots of things—important things."

"I'm going over there right now," Dan said. He dangled a huge, old-fashioned key in front of her nose. "Just to see if it's as bad as I think it is. Want to come along?"

Charli sat up. She'd wanted to go inside the Castle as long as she could remember. "Does Uncle Will know we're going?"

Dan shrugged. "He's out somewhere, and he left the key on the kitchen table. Why would he care?"

They walked down Lincoln toward the gravel lane that led to Barker and the lake beyond. Charli started to say it would be quicker to cut through the woods behind the Crandalls' house and across the field, but she changed her mind. No matter what Dan said about Uncle Will not caring, this inspection was obviously supposed to be a secret.

When they reached the corner, she looked back and saw Sophia come out onto the Crandalls' porch with Mickey in her arms.

"There she is—that Sophia," she said crossly. "She's spying on us."

Dan snorted.

"Well, she might be," Charli insisted. "She looks like a spy."

"Don't be dumb," Dan said.

Charli didn't know how to talk to him when he was like this. She felt like punching him, but he sounded annoyed enough to punch back.

The Castle came into sight, looming over the

row of small houses that faced it. Its tall windows made a pattern of glowing rectangles on either side of the pointed roof. Charli felt a quiver of excitement. Sure the house might look kind of strange, but it was impressive and Uncle Will owned it. *Crandalls' Castle* had a splendid sound.

They walked in silence until they reached the cracked and pitted brick walk that led to the front door. The yard was tufted with weeds, paper scraps, and bits of glass. That would be easy to clean up, Charli told herself, but standing this close to the house she could see paint peeling from the siding and the trim. A broken drainpipe dangled from the eaves, and one of the shutters hung from a single hinge.

Dan groaned. "Man, it's even worse than I remembered!"

"It's not that bad." Charli crossed her fingers. "Uncle Will wouldn't buy it if he didn't know he could fix it up."

"He was sure he could fix up that boat two years ago," Dan reminded her grimly. "Remember how that turned out?"

Charli bit her lip. "Aunt Lilly thinks the bed-and-breakfast is a good idea—"

"She never said so," Dan retorted. "Mom just keeps quiet—it's what she always does when

Dad has a brainstorm. Whatever he wants, that's fine with her. I'm the only one who'll tell him the truth—not that anybody cares what I think!"

Charli felt disloyal listening to this kind of talk. "If you're going inside just so you can find more nasty things to say, I won't go with you," she told him. "You want to hate it!"

"I'm being honest." Dan glared back. "Listen, Charli, the only reason Dad can afford to buy the place is because it's a total dump that nobody else wants. He's using most of his pension money for the down payment, and by the time he finishes his so-called repairs we'll owe everybody in town."

"Not if we all help," Charli argued. "You and I—"

"Count me out," Dan said gruffly. "I've got a job, and if I don't hang on to it I'll never get to college. I probably won't go anyway—we'll have Crandalls' Castle instead!" His voice cracked. "Look, I've changed my mind. You go in if you want—I can see all I need to see right here."

He held out the key, and Charli took it. College, she thought. College was a long way in the future, but it didn't seem so far off to Dan. He couldn't learn to be an engineer without college.

She turned back to the Castle and continued

the argument in her head. It was going to be all right. Uncle Will would make a lot of money with the bed-and-breakfast, and then Dan could go to any college he wanted. The important thing was to get started. . . .

She went up the brick walk but hesitated at the front door. If Heather or Carissa were with her, exploring would be an adventure, but going inside alone was different. She turned the key over uncertainly and then slid it into the keyhole. She had to do it. If she went home now, it would be like admitting Dan was right.

The key turned and she stepped into a dim entranceway tiled in black-and-white squares. Straight ahead, a wide staircase led to the second floor. The wooden steps were dented in the middle like the steps in her school. On either side of the entrance there were long rooms where sunlight lay across the bare floors in dusty patches. The room on the left had a fireplace at the far end, and next to the fireplace there was a chair partly covered by a shabby quilt. The room on the right, probably the dining room, was a little smaller and completely empty.

The air in the old house was stuffy. Charli let the door click shut behind her, shutting out the sound of kids playing across the street. Silence settled around her like a blanket. She crossed the checkered tiles on tiptoe and looked around the living room.

There was no other furniture except the chair, but a window seat stretched below the row of windows facing the street. The room had a funny smell, like dead flowers. Dead something.

She was about to turn back when a movement caught her eye. The expanse of wall opposite the windows was no longer bare. Against the dingy wallpaper lay the shadow of a cradle, as sharply outlined as if it were painted there. Her astonishment deepened to panic as the shadow grew larger and darker. And there was something else. . . .

For a few seconds she was too terrified to move. Then she turned and ran toward the door. The key slipped from her sweaty fingers, but she didn't stop to pick it up. She didn't dare.

She crossed the street, cut between two houses, and was racing across the field toward Uncle Will's house before she let herself think again about what she'd seen.

There was the shadow of a cradle, but no cradle. The shadow had kept growing and darkening. And then it had rocked, as if an invisible hand were moving it.

Chapter Eight
SOPHIA'S JOURNAL

My Crandall bedroom is full of boxes and stuff, but there are two nice big windows. When I go to bed I look out at treetops and stars. Lincoln Street is quiet—nothing like Madison or Sacramento. Of course, the quiet disappears as soon as the sun comes up. Footsteps thump down the stairs, the kids yell, and Will drives off in his old truck with the horn blaring "Yankee Doodle." I dress fast and try to ignore the butterflies flapping around in my stomach. Just be invisible, I tell myself. Watch what you say. Same old thing.

This morning Lilly had already started making sugar cookies when I got downstairs. Her hands darted around, sifting, mixing, rolling out dough, as if they had done it all a thousand times, which I suppose they had. Mickey hung on the leg of her jeans and reached for the mixing bowl until I picked him up. Then he pulled on my braid instead.

"He loves you, Sophia," Lilly said casually, as if it was a little thing. "I think it's remarkable how patient you are with the boys, when you must have a lot on your mind. First your great-grandmother gets sick and then you move here—everything happened so fast. Your head must be whirling."

"I've moved around a lot," I said. "I don't mind."

She looked at me with a doubtful expression. "Well, I hope you'll let us know if there's anything special we can do to make you feel at home while you're here. What would you be doing at home this summer?"

I pressed my face into Mickey's soft curls. "Charli—says we're supposed to help fix up that house you're buying—that Castle." I'd decided I might as well talk about it—let her know how I felt.

She looked startled. "Good heavens, only if you want to do it!" she exclaimed. Her hands flew over the sheet of cookie dough, cutting out stars and diamonds and half-moons. "I know Will has mentioned a job to Charli, but she's alone a lot during the day, and he thought she'd like to earn a little money. You make up your own mind what you want to do."

Since Charli told me we were both going to work for Will this summer, I'd had this tightness in my chest, as if I'd swallowed something that wouldn't go down. The moment she said I could make up my own mind what I wanted to do, the tightness loosened. Lilly couldn't lie if she tried.

"I'd rather help you around the house," I said. "I can look after Mickey and the twins——"

I stopped, jolted by a picture in my mind. The twins were supposed to be in the sandbox, building mountains around the dishpan lake, but the sandbox was empty. I was sure of it, even before I ran to the window with Mickey in my arms.

"You don't have to check on them, dear. Those two won't be satisfied until they've turned all the sand into mountains. They're a lot like their father——determined."

"But they aren't there," I croaked. I dropped Mickey into his high chair and ran down the hall to the front door.

Toys dotted the patch of lawn as usual, but the twins weren't playing with them.

"They're good kids——they never go far," Lilly said behind me. She was trying to reassure both of us.

"I know," I said. I really did know they were close by, but where? Mountains, I thought, and ran across the lawn to the driveway.

The ladder leaned against the side of the house, its top resting against the roof. One of the twins—I was too frightened to be sure which—was three rungs from the top. He stared down at us, his eyes huge in his little face.

Lilly screamed, "Gene, what are you doing?"

"We're climbing a mountain," Terry answered, as if we ought to be able to see that. He was on the ladder, too, but he'd gone up only a couple of steps. "Go," he yelled to his brother. "You're almost to the top!"

Gene didn't move. He was finding out how scary it is to have a lot of empty space below you. I could have told him—I hate high places.

Lilly and I reached the ladder at the same time. She grabbed Terry and swung him away, then I started to climb. It was as if we were a team and didn't need to discuss it.

Terry yelled and struggled to get free, and Gene started to cry. The ladder wobbled under my weight.

"It's okay, Gene," I shouted. "I'm coming up. Hang on tight and take one step down."

"C-Can't," he sobbed. "Can't!"

I felt like crying myself as the ladder shifted some more on the gravel of the driveway.

"He really can't," Lilly said in a low voice. "He's too scared to move." She was trying to steady the ladder with one hand while she held on to Terry with the other.

This is crazy, I thought. I can't do this! We need help. . . . I started to tell Lilly to call the fire department, but I stopped just in time. I didn't want her to let go of the ladder.

So what are you going to do when you get to the top? I asked myself. I couldn't carry Gene, and I couldn't force him to come with me if he didn't want to. He'd have to calm down first, which seemed pretty unlikely, given the way he was crying.

I took a couple more steps and looked up. His little sneakers were just above my head. His fists clutching the side rail were white under a layer of sand. He was flat against the rungs, as if he was glued there.

Two more rungs and I was right behind him. I prayed he wouldn't make a sudden move that would jar us both loose.

"Listen, Gene," I said, "I know a really fun game we can play while we climb down. It's called Simon Says."

He sobbed louder. "Th-that's a dumb game!"

Well, you're right about that, I thought, but it was the best I could do. My brain was a ball of fuzz.

"No, it's not," I said. "Not the way we'll play it. There's a prize if you win. You do whatever I tell you, as long as I say Simon Says first. If I forget to say Simon Says, you *don't* do it. Then you get the prize."

"Wh-what prize?" The question was muffled with tears, but at least he was listening.

I couldn't think, but Lilly could. "A chocolate fudge ice-cream cone, Gene," she called. "Two scoops! Your favorite!"

I touched his ankle. "Simon Says step down with this foot."

He didn't move.

"Come on, Gene, play." I was really begging him now. My knees shook; I felt like throwing up. "Don't forget, two big scoops if you win. Simon Says—"

Very slowly, his left foot dropped down until his toes touched a rung.

"Good, Genie!" Lilly yelled. "That's wonderful." She sounded hysterical.

Before he could change his mind, I went on. "Simon Says step down with the other foot."

He did it, and I moved down with him. "Simon Says slide both hands down a little way."

I held my breath as his fists tightened, loosened, and tightened again. We were actually on our way!

"Simon Says step down with this foot. . . . Simon Says step down with the other foot. . . . Simon Says . . ."

I looked over my shoulder and saw that we were still high enough for a nasty fall. Gene looked down, too, and I could feel him stiffen up again.

"Simon Says move your hands down."

His hands barely moved, and he yelled, "Mommy, I'm scared!" There was so much panic in his voice that I knew the game was over.

I said, "Step down with this foot, Gene." He didn't move, maybe because I hadn't said Simon Says, but more likely because he was too terrified to hear me. It didn't matter which it was.

"Hey, you won!" I said, as excited as I could manage. "You get the prize, Gene! Now just a few more steps—"

But he'd had enough. He crumpled against me so hard that we both started to fall. Lilly screamed and I threw one arm around his waist. For a moment we just hung there. Then I was going down, much too fast because his weight kept me off balance. I missed the last rung completely and sprawled in the driveway. He would have landed on top of me if Lilly hadn't grabbed him as we shot past her.

I was so glad to be back on the ground that I just lay there for a minute and enjoyed it, gravel and all. Lilly was hugging the kids and scolding them at the same time.

"Don't you ever do that again," she said sternly. "Never ever! If Sophia hadn't noticed you were missing—"

"We weren't missing," Terry said. "We were climbing a mountain."

"And I went to the top," Gene said. He was totally pleased with himself. "I was brave."

"Sophia was the brave one, and don't you forget it, young man," Lilly said. "You can thank her right now."

Gene looked down at his shoes.

"Come on, say it," Terry told him. "So we can have the ice cream."

There was a wail from inside the house. "Mickey," I said. "I'll get him."

I ran inside, relieved to get away. If I stuck around, Lilly might ask why I had checked the sandbox when I did. I didn't want any questions.

The rest of the morning was messy and fun and very loud. I'll bet the other customers at Old King

Cone were glad when we finished our ice cream and left, but we didn't care. I guess we all wanted to forget what had just happened—the more noise the better.

A couple of times, I caught Lilly looking at me in a special sort of way, smiling but sort of puzzled, too. Let it go, I thought, please let it go. We were like a family sitting there, and I wanted the feeling to last. A little while longer, at least.

Chapter Nine
CHARLI

"You think I'm fat," Charli said. She tried to make a joke of it, but the words sounded whiny, even to herself.

Ray looked annoyed. "Now that's ridiculous," he said. "You're not fat. I just asked if you wanted to go for a bike ride with me. Your mom won't be home for another hour, and I need some exercise. You can come along if you want to, or you can stay home."

"I'll come," Charli mumbled.

"You don't have to."

"I want to—I guess."

That was the way all their conversations went, she thought unhappily, as she wheeled her bike out of the garage and followed Ray down Lincoln Street. Ever since he moved in, she'd been saying things that irritated him. She had wanted a father. She had wanted *him*, Ray Franz. And now that it had happened, she felt as if he were judging her every minute. If he'd had a daughter of his own, she thought, she would be pretty and skinny and good at everything she tried, especially sports.

"Move, Charli!" He was skimming along ahead of her. "Work up a sweat." As if she weren't already puffing after just a few hundred feet!

They swung around the corner at the end of the street and glided onto the gravel road. Ray gestured across the field toward the Castle. "Crandalls' Castle," he chuckled over his shoulder. "I still can't believe—"

A pickup truck rattled by, drowning out the rest of the sentence, but Charli knew what he couldn't believe. She had heard him tell her mother that Will was making a terrible mistake and they should all try to talk him out of it. Her mother hadn't said much, but Charli could tell she was worried.

She slowed down a little so she wouldn't be expected to talk. She wanted to defend Uncle Will, but at the same time she, too, wished he would forget about Crandalls' Castle. The rocking shadow-cradle was never far from her thoughts. She had even dreamed about it. There had been something deeply menacing about that slow, unstoppable movement.

Ray turned onto the lake road and waited for her to catch up. Farther down, cottages lined the shore, but first came a wide strip of pale sand that stretched in a half-moon around the bay.

"Why would anyone want to go to a water park when they could swim in a beautiful place like this?" Ray wondered aloud. He stopped pedaling to stare across the water, and Charli braked next to him.

"We ought to come over here to swim once in a while," he went on. "Do you know how to swim, Charli?"

"Sort of," Charli said. "I paddle."

"We can work on that," he told her. "Everyone should know how to swim."

Charli felt warmed by more than the late-afternoon sun, but then he spoiled the moment by saying, "Maybe that kid who moved in with Will and Lilly—what's her name, Sophie? Maybe she'd like to come with us."

"Sophia," Charli said. "I don't know if she likes swimming."

Ray shrugged and got back on his bike. "Can't hurt to ask," he said. "She's probably lonesome."

"How can she be lonesome?" Charli demanded. "She's got a whole crowd of people around her all the time."

Ray didn't answer, and they finished the ride in silence. *Now he thinks I'm mean,* she thought. *He probably expected she and Sophia would become best friends just because they lived across the street from each other.*

"Sophia doesn't like me," she told him as they wheeled their bikes up the driveway.

Ray glanced at her. "How do you know that?"

"I just know. She thinks I have dumb ideas."

She hurried into the house before he could ask any more questions, aware that the bicycle ride was ending as sourly as it had begun.

They had spaghetti with meatballs for dinner, Charli's favorite food. Rona told them about some Japanese tourists whose bus had stopped at the restaurant on their way to see the Mississippi River. The visitors had spoken Japanese among themselves, but they all knew English words for *hamburgers* and *french fries* because they ate at McDonald's at home. Then Ray described the bike ride and how beautiful the lake had looked. He seemed to be waiting for Charli to add something, but she kept her head down and ate steadily. Afterward, she rinsed off the plates, put them into the dishwasher, and escaped to the front porch.

Dan was in the middle of the street, rescuing a ball the twins had thrown there. When he saw Charli he told the boys to take the ball around to the backyard to play. Then he joined her on the front steps.

"You look pretty grumpy," he commented. "Or is that just your real self shining through?"

Charli made a face at him. "You're pretty grumpy sometimes yourself," she snapped. "I ought to know!"

"I told you I was sorry about the other day," Dan said. "When I looked at that old barn up close and thought about all the money that was going to be spent on it—" He broke off and grinned at her. "At least I didn't leave the key on the floor," he teased.

"Don't laugh," Charli said hotly. "I had a good reason for not going back."

"What reason?"

"You wouldn't believe me," she said. "It's too weird."

"Try me." He leaned back and stretched out his long legs.

Charli hesitated. She had wanted very much to tell someone what she'd seen in the living room at the Castle, but so far she hadn't. The grown-ups in her family would just laugh and say she had a great imagination. Ray would probably think she was being silly.

"Promise not to tell Ray or my mom," she said sternly. "*Really* promise."

"Okay."

Charli took a deep breath. "I went in the house and it was spooky, but I went into one of the rooms anyway. . . ." Then the words tumbled out. The shadow on the wall . . . the moment when the shadow started rocking as if someone were pushing it . . . the terror that had made her drop the key and run out of the house.

When she'd finished she looked at Dan to see if he was laughing. "It's true!" she told him fiercely. "You'd better believe me!"

Dan nodded. "Okay," he said. "But for Pete's sake, don't tell any of that to my dad. He'll want the old wreck more than ever if he thinks it's haunted."

"I know." Charli remembered Uncle Will saying people would love to stay in a haunted house. "But I can't work there," she went on miserably. "I just can't. So what am I going to say if he asks me again?"

"Tell him you're busy."

"Who'd believe I'm busy! My mom will think I ought to help, and Ray will say I need the exercise."

"You do," Dan said crushingly and laughed as she tried to push him off the step. "Look." He was suddenly serious. "If you want, I'll go over there with you when I get home from work tomorrow. Maybe I can figure out what you saw."

Charli cringed.

"Oh, come on, goofy," he urged. "If we don't go, you're going to keep right on worrying. For nothing!"

She thought it over. Dan was being a smart aleck, treating her as if she were a silly little kid. Still, it was nice of him to offer to go with her. She knew he didn't want anything to do with the Castle.

"Well?" When she continued to hesitate he grinned slyly. "I can ask Sophia the Silent to go with me if you won't. I bet she can find an answer for you."

That did it! "I'll go," Charli said with a shudder. "Just you and me."

Chapter Ten

CHARLI

❧

In twenty-four hours Charli changed her mind about going back to the Castle at least twenty-four times. She knew what she had seen there—why get scared to death again? Still, if Dan could find an explanation for the shadow, she would feel a lot more cheerful than she did now.

She was still arguing with herself when her tall cousin rounded the corner onto Lincoln Street, walking fast. "I'll see if Dad left the key," he called across the street. "You wait here."

She felt a surge of hope. Maybe Uncle Will had taken the key with him. Then she wouldn't have to go today, and Dan couldn't invite Sophia in her place. She stared at the Crandalls' front door, fingers crossed, until he appeared and signaled her to follow him around the side of the house.

"We'll go through the backyard and cut across the field," he said when she caught up. "Nobody will notice. My mom's out, and Sophia has the kids down in the basement playing. Sounds like they're having a ball."

They plunged into the patch of woods at the end of the yard. "What's your big hurry?" Charli demanded. "It won't be dark for hours."

Dan stopped so suddenly that she almost crashed into him. "Look, I promised I'd do this, so I'm doing it," he said impatiently. "But my mom left a note telling me to baby-sit the kids as soon as I got home from work. She doesn't want Sophia to think she has to take care of them full-time."

Sophia again. Charli longed to tell him to forget the whole thing, but he strode off before she had a chance.

On the far side of the field they cut between two houses, ignoring the curious stare of a woman digging weeds in her yard. While Dan fitted the key into the Castle door, Charli peeked over her shoulder and saw that the woman had come around her house to watch them.

"She thinks we're breaking in," she muttered.

Dan snorted. "So what? I bet she doesn't care

one way or the other. She'd probably be grateful if we burned the place down. Who'd want to look out their front window at this dump all day?"

He pushed open the door and they stepped into the musty foyer.

"In there," Charli whispered, pointing. They crossed to the archway and looked into the long narrow room.

"Right there." She gestured at the bare wall opposite the windows. "In the middle."

"Well, it's not there now," Dan said. "And there's nothing across from it that could make a shadow. No way!"

Charli bit her lip. "Wait a minute. The shadow wasn't there the first time I looked in here. It just—came."

"You imagined it," Dan said. Now he sounded bored. "The trouble with you is, you *want* to see a ghost."

"No, I don't!" Charli protested. "Maybe I did once, but I don't now. That chair next to the fireplace," she added desperately. "It looks different."

"Different how?"

"I don't know," she admitted. "It's changed since I was here the first time, that's all."

Dan groaned. "Cut it out, will you? This is a

waste of time, Charli. Either you're trying to scare yourself, or"—he paused—"maybe you'd rather lie around and read all summer instead of helping out here." His face reddened at her expression, but he kept on. "That won't work, and you'd better believe it. My dad would put out the welcome mat for a ghost, and your folks—Ray, especially—would tell you to quit goofing off and get busy."

"But I don't want to goof off!" Charli was so angry she could hardly speak. "You think you know *everything*! I did see that shadow, I don't care what you say—"

She broke off. Someone else was talking.

"Hey!" Dan exclaimed. They went back into the foyer and stared up at the staircase. The soft murmuring continued. It was a woman's voice, speaking in a singsong rhythm that reminded Charli of the verses she used to chant when she jumped rope.

"Told you so!" She mouthed the words at Dan, but he shook his head impatiently.

"Don't be dumb, that's no ghost. Somebody's broken in—a homeless person—maybe a runaway. She's probably been hanging out here and nobody's noticed."

"But why is she singing?"

"Thinks she's going to scare us off," Dan muttered. He started up the stairs. "Well, it's not going to work."

"It works for me," Charli protested. "Whoever she is, she sounds really strange. What if she has a gun or a knife? Let's go! We can call the police from your house." She tugged at Dan's sleeve, but he shook her off.

"Go if you want to," he said. "She might get away before the police come, and then we'll never know whether . . ."

Whether she's real or not, Charli thought. Dan wasn't as sure of the truth as he pretended to be.

At the top of the stairs they stopped to listen. The landing was deep enough to be used as a small sitting room. On either side of it extended a hallway lined with doors, some open, some closed.

The voice was louder up here. "That way," Charli whispered, wondering if she was the only one who thought the song sounded unreal, more like an echo than a real voice. She glanced at Dan and saw his eyes widen in alarm.

They started down the hallway, stopping to peek into each room. Except for an old chest in one room and a chair with a broken rocker in another, there was little to see but dusty floors and stained, peeling wallpaper. The bathroom held a huge, grimy-looking tub, and there was a partly closed door that turned out to be a linen cabinet. At each doorway, Charli's heart beat faster and the singing grew louder.

"In there," Dan said. He nodded at a closed door at the end of the hall. "Has to be."

Another sound began then, a soft gurgling.

"Hey, that's a baby!" Charli whispered. "She has a baby with her." Maybe Dan was right; a homeless person had sneaked into the Castle . . . a mother who needed help . . . no one to be afraid of. . . .

The singing stopped, and laughter took its place. Mothers laugh with their babies, Charli reminded herself; mothers sing and laugh—only not like this. The laughter swirled around them like the shriek of a bird. Charli gasped as the baby began to scream.

The last door was open a crack. Dan kicked it hard and as it swung back the laughter and the screams stopped.

Charli peered around his shoulder. "Where are they?" she whispered. "Where's the baby?"

He gave the door another shove, and now they could see the entire room. It was empty except for a bed. In the middle of the sagging mattress was a faded quilt, oddly bunched.

"Nobody," Dan said, breathing hard. "There's nobody here at all!"

Charli turned and ran, half-falling down the staircase and out the big front door. She didn't know if Dan was behind her until she heard the door close and the key turn in the lock.

When she slowed to walk, at last, she was halfway across the field. Dan caught up to her, his hands shoved in his pockets.

"I said I didn't want to stay long, and we sure didn't," he said dryly. "I never saw you move so fast."

She glared at him. "I suppose you aren't as scared as I am," she snapped. "I suppose you think there was a real woman and a real baby in that room. Hiding in the closet or something!"

"There aren't any closets," Dan said. "Didn't you notice? That house was built when people hung their clothes in wardrobes. Which is another great thing for my dad to keep in mind when he thinks about furnishing all those bedrooms."

"But he *won't* furnish them," Charli said, shocked. "Not when we tell him—"

"We're not going to tell him," Dan said flatly.

"At least, I'm not going to. What's the point? If there's one thing that would make him even more determined to go ahead it would be to hear that the Castle is haunted. He'd put an ad in the papers, for Pete's sake: 'Spend the night in a genuine haunted house. Ghost guaranteed, one to a customer!'"

Charli groaned. "But he wants me to help," she wailed. "I can't work there!"

Dan walked faster.

"Could they have been behind the door?" she demanded desperately. "A lady and her baby? Is that possible?"

"No, it isn't," Dan said gruffly. "Maybe someone was playing a trick on us—who knows?" Then, as if he were reading her mind, he closed off the only escape route she had. "If you're smart you won't tell Aunt Rona about this either," he said. "She'd probably try to help—tell my dad she's decided you shouldn't work this summer or something—but she'd tell Ray about it, too. And I can guess what he'd say about people who believe in ghosts."

Chapter Eleven
SOPHIA'S JOURNAL

Dan calls the twins' mountain-climbing adventure a Crandall Moment. That's how his family lives, he says, one near-disaster after another, *especially his dad*. If that's so, then I guess they already understand that Will is a dangerous person. But they don't know how dangerous, and neither do I. I keep waiting for a sign.

I've had some Crandall Moments of my own, but they aren't disasters—just neat memories I'll take with me if I have to leave here next week or next month. Whenever. Yesterday, when I called Mickey and held out my arms, he took three or four steps before he toppled over! And last night I discovered Lilly had put her mother's hand-stitched spread on my bed. I could hardly believe it. If I had something my mother made, I'd keep it locked up in a safe.

And then today. For some reason I slept through all the morning clatter, and when I finally went downstairs Lilly and Will and the kids were nearly through eating breakfast. I smelled warm cinnamon rolls and—this is strange—it made me think again of my mother. Actually, I don't remember her at all, but for a few seconds I felt as if I did.

I must have looked happy, because Will said, "Hey, Sophia's smiling," as if that was a big deal. Dan pushed the rolls toward my chair and said, "You'd better grab one while you have a chance. You're lucky the monsters left any for you."

"Not a monster," Gene shouted. "I only had two. Terry had three and a half."

Terry yelled, "Didn't," and a battle began. Mickey cried.

Will said, "Shame on you kids, you've scared the baby," but Lilly laughed. "He needs a clean diaper, poor dear," she said. "I'll take him." She stood up and looked at her noisy kids as if all that racket was music to her.

Dan rolled his eyes and said, "Time to go to work, thank goodness!" And Lilly laughed some more. As they walked down the hall together, I heard her say, "You were just as bad when you were their age, and look at you now." You could tell he's absolutely perfect in her eyes—they all are.

With no one but Will and me left to listen, the twins quieted down. Then Terry smiled, which really does make him look like an angel, and said, "Let's play hide-and-seek. That would be fun."

I said, "Okay, soon as I have my breakfast," and the smile disappeared.

"Not you, Sophia—Daddy," he said. "We want Daddy."

Will looked pleased. "Okay," he said. "Ten minutes, no more. You go out in the backyard and wait until Sophia calls you to come in." He winked at me as if he liked hide-and-seek as much as they did.

The twins dashed out the back door, and—well, you won't believe what happened after that. Will kicked off his shoes and went into the pantry, which is a long, narrow closet-room with cupboards and a counter, and shelves that go nearly to the ceiling. For a second or two he stared at the shelves, and then he climbed onto the counter in his stocking feet. He began taking canisters and boxes and jars from the top shelf, his long arms swooping down to the counter, up and down, up and down, like a robot's.

"Been thinking about this ever since the last

time we played," he panted. "You'll see—it'll drive the kids crazy!"

It drove me crazy, just watching him. In no time, he'd made a total mess of the pantry, piling boxes in teetery stacks and shoving cans to the back of the counter with his feet. I thought, What will Lilly say? What would my great-grandmother say if she saw him, or Mrs. Wagner? Why was he doing it, anyway?

I found out why, soon enough. When the top shelf was empty, he stepped onto a big box labeled cookbooks and climbed from there to the edge of the first shelf. Then he sort of chinned himself on the top shelf and swung upward. It sounds impossible, but the next thing I knew he was stretched out almost full length on the highest shelf. Only his blue-jeaned knees stuck out over the edge.

"Okay, Sophia," he called. "Tell them they can come in."

Lilly came back to the kitchen with Mickey just as the twins threw open the screen door and raced around. They looked under the table and in the broom closet and then tore into the dining room and up the stairs, making enough noise for ten.

Lilly said, "Uh-oh, hide-and-seek," as if she'd seen this before. "Where . . . ?"

Now comes the explosion, I thought. I nodded toward the pantry and held my breath.

Her big eyes widened when she saw the clutter of boxes and jars and cans on the counter. "Oh, Will," she groaned, and Will peeked over the edge of the top shelf. He looked really pleased with himself.

"You are out of your mind," she said. Then she giggled!

He made a shushing sound and moved out of sight, because the twins were clattering back down the stairs. When they burst into the kitchen, their faces were red with excitement.

"Are we warm or cold?" Gene demanded. "If Daddy's in the basement, that's not fair."

Lilly said, "You're warm. Especially you, Terry. Oh, you're very, very, very warm!"

Gene ran to the pantry door and pushed Terry out of the way.

"He's not in here," he yelled. "There's nobody in here, Mama. You shouldn't say that—"

"Look!" Terry pointed up at the blue knees poking over the edge of the top shelf. "I found him!" he yelled. "He's right there!"

Will's long legs shot out over the edge of the shelf. His feet danced in the air like a puppet's until they settled on the box of cookbooks.

"You both found me!" he shouted. "What a pair

of detectives!" Then he was back on the floor, gathering up the boys in his arms and hoisting one to each shoulder. He grinned at Lilly and me and headed out the back door, his knees bent in a kind of duckwalk so the kids wouldn't bump their heads.

When they were gone the kitchen was awfully quiet. Lilly put Mickey in his high chair and picked up Will's shoes from under the table. There was a hole in the sole of one of them.

"Look at that," she said, shaking her head. "He should get this fixed. I keep telling him, but he never has time."

"I'll put that stuff back on the shelf," I told her. "It won't take long."

She looked confused, as if she'd forgotten the mess in there. "That would be nice," she said. "Will could do it later, but . . ." Her voice sort of trailed off and she smiled, a wonderful, dreamy kind of smile. "You know, it's not a big deal, Sophia. Which do you think Gene and Terry will remember longer—a nice, neat pantry or finding their daddy tucked up there on that shelf? Just imagine how they'll laugh about it twenty years from now. They'll probably tell their kids about the funny things their grandpa did."

I've never heard anyone talk like that before. Not the Stengels or the Wagners, or anyone else

I've lived with. They talked about work and about money, and I guess they made jokes once in a while, but I don't remember them.

"Will wants to get started over at the Castle today," Lilly said. "He's going to ask if you'd like to help—he'd pay you, of course. I just want to be sure you understand you don't have to do it, Sophia. When he gets excited about a project, he assumes everyone else is as thrilled as he is. They sometimes aren't, but that enthusiasm is one of the things I love most about him."

I'd already made up my mind not to work at the Castle—I told you that. I don't want to spend a lot of time with Charli. I don't like the looks of that creepy old house. I'm worried about Will. None of that had changed, but somehow it didn't matter right then. I guess I was having a Crandall Moment of my own because I said, "It's okay. I'll help." I want to feel like a part of the family in every way I can, for as long as they'll let me.

Chapter Twelve
CHARLI

"Uncle Will is going to start working over at the Castle today," Charli's mother said. "He called before you got up to see if you were ready."

For the first time in her life Charli was glad she had a dentist's appointment.

"I can't," she said quickly. "I have to see Dr. Geder, remember?"

"What about this afternoon, then?" her mother said. "You could go for a couple of hours, couldn't you? Just to show we support him."

"But do we want to support him?" Ray asked, looking up from the morning paper. "As far as I'm concerned, he's making the biggest mistake of his life."

Good! Charli thought. He's taking my side.

Then he spoiled it by adding, "But you need *something* to do this summer, Charli. I suppose helping Will is better than nothing."

"Sophia's going to be there," her mother added. "That should be more fun than working by yourself."

They were ganging up on her—her mother, Ray, Uncle Will, even Miss Perfect Sophia, who was willing to help when Uncle Will's own niece would rather go to the dentist.

"That old house is scary." She had to say it. "I hate it!"

Her mother looked surprised, and Ray stared at her. "Scary?" He repeated the word slowly, as if he'd never heard it before. "How old are you, Charli, my girl? Do you really believe every old house is scary?"

"No, not every one," she began. The words faded under Ray's disapproving look. "Ask Dan," she tried again. "We heard voices upstairs, and I saw a shadow—"

Ray shook his head. "Please spare me," he said. "I don't want to hear about it."

"Just give it a try, dear," Rona suggested. "You love Uncle Will. . . ."

"Love has nothing to do with it," Ray interrupted. "You know I think that so-called Castle is a lost cause, but at least it will give Charli something to do. I hate to see her lying around watching TV and reading all summer. She needs exercise." Then he clapped his hands and grinned. "End of lecture," he said briskly. "Do you want a ride to the dentist's office, Charli?"

"I'll take my bike," Charli said. "For exercise." She suspected the "lecture" might begin again in the car.

It was after two before she finally ran out of excuses and set off for the Castle—the long way. As soon as she turned onto the lake road she could see Uncle Will out in front of the house, picking up scraps of paper and soda cans and dropping them into one of the two trash bags he dragged behind him. When he saw her, he dropped the bags and waved both arms in welcome.

"I can do that," she called. She'd much rather pick up trash than go inside.

Uncle Will shook his head. "I'll be through with this in a few minutes, and then I'm going to cut the grass," he told her. "Sophia's sweeping. The floors have to be refinished some day, but right now we'll have to settle for a good cleaning." He looked at the Castle proudly. "Just think how wonderful it's going to look when all those dirty windows are shining, Charli. I'm going to plant flowers on either side of the steps, and some shrubs, too. Before you know it people will be lining up to invest money in the place. Won't that be terrific?"

Charli tried to see the Castle the way Uncle Will was seeing it. When he was excited, he was awfully convincing—if you didn't know what Ray and Dan thought about the Castle.

"There's soda in a cooler in the kitchen," he called as she started up the steps. "Take all the breaks you want."

The heavy front door was propped open with a brick. Charli stepped inside and looked quickly up the stairs.

"I've just started to mop," Sophia said. She was in the dining room, looking as if she knew exactly how scared Charli was and thought it was a big joke. "There's another mop and a bucket in the kitchen."

Bossy! Charli grumbled to herself as she went down the hall to the big, old-fashioned kitchen. But she had to admit her mother had been right; it was going to be easier working in the Castle with another person close by. Even Sophia.

There was floor cleaner in a box of supplies on the counter, and soon she was sloshing sudsy water across the living-room floor. She had never mopped a floor before, and she wondered if there was a right way to do it. If there was, she was sure Sophia would tell her. With each stroke she glanced at the wall opposite the windows, in case the shadow-cradle reappeared. She almost wished it would, so that Sophia could see it, too. Maybe then she'd be sorry she'd called Charli childish for believing in ghosts.

A half hour dragged by. Charli went out to the kitchen to fill the pail with fresh water. When she returned, Sophia met her in the hall.

"Your uncle's calling you."

Charli dropped the bucket and dashed out the door, grateful for the chance to get out of the house. Uncle Will was leaning out the window of his truck.

"Look up there, kiddo," he shouted. "Second floor, fourth window from the end."

Charli looked where he was pointing. Her heart thumped at the thought of what she might see, but there was nothing in the window at all.

"How about that!" Uncle Will exclaimed. "Must be dozens of 'em!"

Charli squinted. Insects crawled around the window frame and hovered near the glass.

"Wasps!" Uncle Will announced. "I just

noticed 'em. I'm going into town for more trash bags and some geraniums, and I'll pick up spray if we need it. Run upstairs and see if there's a nest between the storm window and the inside pane."

"Upstairs?" Charli choked on the word. "I— I can't—"

"You can't?" Uncle Will cocked his head at her. "You feeling okay, Charli?"

She hesitated. Another second and he might decide she was sick and send her home. He would tell her mother. Her mother would tell Ray. The whole family would know she'd refused to go upstairs in the Castle and would want to know why.

"Okay," she said hoarsely. She ran back into the house before he could ask any more questions.

"He wants me to look for a wasps' nest," she told Sophia. "Upstairs."

Sophia looked at her closely. "Are you afraid of wasps? They won't hurt you if you don't get too close."

"I'm not afraid of wasps," Charli said. Now she really did feel sick.

"Well, then."

Of course! Wonderful, brave Sophia wasn't afraid of wasps, or of ghosts, either. Charli started up the stairs, her feet so heavy it was hard to lift them.

"I'll go, too," Sophia offered, suddenly at her side. "I haven't seen the upstairs."

Charli let out her breath. She climbed faster to keep up with Sophia's quick steps. When they reached the landing, Sophia started to turn right, but Charli grabbed her wrist with sweating fingers.

"Not there," she whispered, terrified that the singing might start again. "It's this way, fourth window from the end."

They walked down the hall together, glancing through doorways. There were two windows in each room, spreading sunlight across the bare floors in dusty rectangles. When they reached the third bedroom, they could see the small black bodies that darted between the panes.

Sophia crossed to the window. "There's a nest all right," she said. "A big one. Want to see?"

"No!" Charli said. "I'll tell Uncle Will." She ran back to the stairs, her eyes on the closed door at the other end of the hall.

It wasn't until she reached the front door that she realized she was alone. Sophia was still on the top step, looking from side to side and frowning.

"What's wrong?" Charli asked. "What are you looking at?"

Sophia gave her head a little shake, as if she were waking from a dream. She started down the steps. "I'm not looking at anything," she said. "What is there to see?"

Chapter Thirteen
SOPHIA'S JOURNAL

Charli nagged all the way home from the Castle. I take bigger steps than she does, but she ran to keep up. "You did see something upstairs. What was it? Why did you get that look on your face?"

I said, "I don't know what you're talking about," but she didn't believe me. And she could get me in trouble, the way Linda Wagner did.

"What do you think I saw?" I tried to make it sound like a joke. "Besides a dusty hallway."

"A ghost," she said. "I bet you saw a ghost."

"Well, I didn't," I told her. "What's wrong with you, anyway? If you go around telling people the house is haunted, you'll make your uncle feel bad. He loves that place, in case you haven't noticed."

"Uncle Will wouldn't care," she said. "Dan says Uncle Will thinks people would pay more to spend the night in a haunted house."

She's probably right, I thought. Will Crandall would welcome a ghost. But I know he wouldn't welcome being told Crandalls' Castle is an awful place. He'd say, "What makes you say a thing like that, Sophia?" And I'd say, "When I went upstairs I had the same feeling I had the day my school burned in Sacramento." Then he'd say, "What are you talking about?" I'd have to tell him. . . .

I don't want to think about it. The way he'd look at me, wondering what kind of nut he had staying at his house! The way Lilly would look at me—like, why is this weird, ungrateful kid trying to make my Will unhappy?

"Just leave me out of it," I told Charli. "I don't like ghost stories." We had reached the woods at the end of the Crandalls' yard. I rushed ahead and up the back steps before she could ask any more questions.

I wanted to come up here to my bedroom and think for a while, before I had to talk to anyone else, but no luck. Lilly was at the stove, stirring tomato sauce with a long spoon and helping Mickey stand up with the other hand. I grabbed him just as he was about to fall.

"Sophia to the rescue as usual," Lilly said. "You look tired, dear. Did Will work you girls too hard?"

"No way." I whirled around the kitchen with Mickey in my arms to prove I wasn't tired at all.

"I thought Will would be home by now," she said, laughing at us. "We'll eat as soon as he comes."

I told her he had gone downtown for spray to get rid of a big wasps' nest at the Castle.

She nodded and said something that really surprised me. "You know, I still haven't been inside that house. I've passed it for years, of course, but now we own it and I should go in and look around but . . ."

"Why don't you?" I said.

She gave the sauce an extra hard stir. "Well," she said, "I realize it's very run-down, and I don't have Will's knack for seeing how things will turn out. Sometimes I just see the down side, and that makes me a terrible wet blanket. So I don't interfere. Will knows what he needs to do . . . he's a very hard worker . . . he . . ." She turned away from the stove, and I thought her face looked strained. But maybe I imagined it, because she smiled and said, "Will figures out how to support this lively family, and I take care of us at home. That's the way we both like it."

I put Mickey in the high chair and started taking

plates and glasses from the cupboard. How can she be so sure Will is doing the right thing when I know absolutely, positively, this time he's WRONG? The trouble is, he can be wrong and never have to admit it, even to himself. *That's what makes him dangerous.*

I thought about the Castle all through dinner and the twins' spaghetti-slurping contest. I couldn't stop thinking about it. The first floor is bad enough, but the second floor is worse. I didn't see a ghost up there, even though Charli is sure I did. I didn't *see anything.* I just knew I wouldn't spend a night in one of those rooms for a million dollars.

Charli was in the truck when Will and I came out of the house this morning. She looked at me hard, but I didn't look back.

"You ladies have a short workday today," Will said. "How about getting started in the kitchen this morning? In a week or so I'd like to invite some big-money folks to look around—let them see how nice the Castle's going to be. Do what you can before eleven—I hear you have other plans for this afternoon."

"What plans?" I asked.

Will looked at Charli, but she was very busy fastening her seat belt. Finally she said, "My mom has the day off, and we're going to the mall. Ray says you should come with us."

I could tell from the way she said it what she thought of that idea.

"I can't," I said. "Lilly might want me to——"

"Lilly wants you to have a good time," Will interrupted. "So do I. You can't work all the time, girl. Go and enjoy yourself."

I was just going to tell him I'd rather enjoy myself at home with Mickey, but then the truck bounced in and out of a pothole with a jolt that sent things flying off the dashboard. A book tumbled out of the glove compartment and landed in my lap.

"Hey, I'd forgotten that book," Will said, so pleased you'd think he hit the pothole on purpose. "The real estate lady gave it to me when we closed the deal on the house. William Herndon's story of his life. He was born in the Castle and lived there till he was two or three years old. She thought we might want to put up a plaque in the living room or something."

Charli asked, "Who's William Herndon?" She sounded about as interested as she did when she told me I was invited to go to the mall, but Will didn't notice.

"Just a former governor of the state," he said.

"How about that—a governor born in Crandalls' Castle!"

Charli shrugged. I wasn't much interested either. I was thinking about this afternoon. Charli didn't want me along. I didn't want to go. As far as I was concerned, it was one more time when I might say something that would get me into trouble.

When we reached the Castle, Will gave me the front door key and Charli a cooler. "Lemonade and cookies," he said. "Made the lemonade myself. I'm going to work on the shutters out here—see if I can straighten them."

I'd guessed we'd have to clean up that old kitchen sooner or later, but I wasn't looking forward to it. The refrigerator wouldn't be so bad, and the gas range—an old-fashioned one on high legs—would probably clean up okay, but the wood-burning stove was a disaster. It looked like a huge sooty bullfrog crouched against the wall.

Charli groaned and said, "What a mess!"

"Let's do the fridge and the gas stove first," I said. "I'll ask Lilly tonight what we should use on the woodstove."

She didn't argue, just began filling the buckets with hot water. Then she went over to the refrigerator and wrote her name on the door with a wet finger. I started on the gas stove. We didn't talk, but I knew she was watching me.

"You'll never get the gook out from under those burners," she said after a while.

I grabbed a grate and tugged until it came loose, sending a shower of old crumbs to the floor.

"Nothing to it," I said. "I'll soak the grates in the sink and wipe up what was underneath them. My great-grandmother had a stove like this one."

She went back to washing the refrigerator. I'll say this for her, she worked hard—took out all the shelves and the drawers and scrubbed them. If Will ever turns this place into a bed-and-breakfast, he'll probably need a new fridge and a new stove, too, but by the time we finished, the old ones looked as good as possible.

The cupboards were next—tall with glass doors. We'd need a ladder for the top shelves.

Charli said, "I'll tell Uncle Will." She ran down the hall to the front door, like a kid let out of school.

When she came back, about five minutes later, she had a little boy with her.

"The short ladder's at home," she said. "Uncle Will's going to get it. This is Jake. We're supposed to give him lemonade."

"I was helping," the boy said. "I handed him

nails and stuff." He took the paper cup of lemonade Charli poured for him and looked around.

"This is a big house," he said, in case we hadn't
noticed.

I asked him where he lived, and he pointed
toward the street. "Over there," he said. "Our house
is little. You're lucky."

Charli said, "It's not our house—it belongs to
my uncle, the man on the ladder. We work for him."

He said, "Can I go upstairs?" and she yelled,
"No!" so loudly that Jake and I both jumped.

"Why not?"

Charli scowled at him. "You just can't, that's
all. My uncle doesn't want kids running around up
there."

Jake said, "I'm not kids—I'm one kid. I
wouldn't hurt anything."

"Drink your lemonade," Charli told him. "You
can look around down here if you want to, but if you
go upstairs, I'll call my uncle and you'll be sorry."

He wandered out of the kitchen and down the
hall, carrying the cup of lemonade in both hands.
Charli didn't look at me, and I knew she was afraid
I'd ask what was so special about upstairs. For the
first time I wondered if she had good reasons of
her own for being afraid of this house. Up till
then I'd assumed she just liked the idea of a ghost

and was hoping I—or someone—would back her up.

We filled our pails with fresh water and started washing down the battered old chairs that stood around the table. Charli kept glancing at the kitchen door, waiting for Jake to come back. When he returned to the kitchen, she looked relieved.

This time he ignored her and walked around the table to where I was working. "Who's that other lady?" he asked. His eyes were very big in his grimy face. "Does she work here, too? Is she your boss?"

I asked, "What other lady?"

Charli made a funny little noise in her throat. "There isn't any other lady," she said. "Don't lie!"

Jake looked at her scornfully and marched back down the hall, slopping lemonade with every step.

"She's right in here," he yelled from the front hall. Then he stopped and looked back to where we were watching him from the kitchen. "Well, she was here before," he said. "She was sitting in the chair with the blanket on her lap. She smiled at me."

I followed him down the hall, with Charli behind me. We all stared at the chair by the living-room fireplace. I thought Charli would bawl him out again for lying, but she just stood there.

"There wasn't anybody else here, Jake," I told

him. "You made that up. You shouldn't try to scare people."

I wasn't scolding, just trying to calm him down, but he'd had enough of us. "I'm not telling lies, you are!" he yelled. He threw his paper cup onto our nice clean floor and ran out the front door.

I didn't know what to make of it, and I still don't, but Jake's imaginary lady sure made an impression on Charli. I asked her if she'd told Jake that the Castle was haunted, but she shook her head.

"Because if you did, that explains what he thinks he saw," I told her. "He's too little to know what's real and what isn't."

"I didn't tell him anything," she said. She looked as if she was in a trance.

"Well, forget it then," I said. "He's just a baby." I wanted to make her feel better, but it didn't work.

"That thing on the chair—he called it a blanket," she whispered. "That's a patchwork quilt. I saw it before, upstairs in the last bedroom. All crumpled up in the middle of the bed. How did it get down here?"

Chapter Fourteen

CHARLI

Dan was sitting on the front steps when Charli came around the side of the Crandalls' house. "Go on inside and get a cinnamon roll," he suggested. "You look as if you need it."

"I'm not hungry," Charli lied. She was starving, but Sophia was already in the house, receiving a noisy welcome home from Mickey and Aunt Lilly.

"Wait'll I tell you what just happened," Charli said. "Remember the ghost we heard singing in the Castle—well, she was in the living room this morning! Sitting in that old chair next to the fireplace."

Dan narrowed his eyes. "You saw her?"

"I didn't see her, but Jake did—he's a little boy

who lives across the street. She smiled at him!"
Charli waited. "Isn't that just unbelievable?"

Dan laughed. "Definitely unbelievable. Kids
make up stuff, Charli. *You* make up stuff. Kids in
this neighborhood have been talking about
ghosts in that old wreck for years."

"But there really is a ghost!" Charli exclaimed,
outraged. "You know there is—we heard it."

Dan stood up and stretched. "At this point I
don't know what we heard," he said. "It was
weird all right, but I don't spend a lot of time
wondering about it. I've got more important
things on my mind."

"Like what?" Charli demanded.

"Like looking for a second job. Like keeping
my grades up enough to get a scholarship."

Charli groaned. Money for college was all he
thought about these days. Talk about Crandalls'
Castle just made him angry.

"Go get a cinnamon roll," he advised again as
he reached for his bike. "And for Pete's sake, get
off the ghost kick. Why make things worse than
they already are?"

"You sound just like Sophia," Charli told him.
"So—so darned superior! Like you're a hundred
years older than I am and know everything."

"Well, you can use a lot of help," her cousin

teased. "And Sophia's okay. She likes to help people, so enjoy it." Then he was gone, gliding swiftly down the street on his battered bike.

Enjoy it! Charli grumbled under her breath. What exactly was she supposed to enjoy? If things were the way they used to be, she'd be with Aunt Lilly right now. Or Aunt Lilly might be out here on the porch with a whole plateful of cinnamon rolls. They'd be having a feast, just the two of them. Aunt Lilly had forgotten all about her niece who loved her.

Sighing, Charli trudged across the street to take a shower and have a sandwich before her mother and Ray came home from work. Her mother had said they would leave for the mall as soon as she and Sophia were ready.

I'll be ready, Charli thought sourly. I'll be ready, but Sophia may be too busy talking to Aunt Lilly.

An hour into the visit to the mall, Charli discovered she was having fun. One reason was that Ray liked to buy things. Her mother treated most stores like museums: places where you looked and admired but didn't buy, unless there was a sale. Ray was different. When Charli admired an apple green top, he held it up in front of her to study the effect. And then he bought it. By three-thirty she had two new tops with pants to match, Sophia had a reddish orange sweater that looked great with her dark hair, and Rona had a long blue skirt that swirled around her ankles. When they stopped at the Jungle House for a snack, the hostess had to help them stow all their bundles under the table.

"This is what happens when you're a family man," Ray said. He winked at Charli in a way that told her he liked the feeling.

The chocolate malts at the Jungle House were perfect—tall and gooey, with extra ice cream at the bottom. Charli waited for Ray to say she should have something less fattening, but he didn't. He didn't even look disapproving when she ordered the Super Dooper.

"Anything goes today," he announced grandly. "What would you like, Sophia?"

"A strawberry sundae," Sophia said at once. "Strawberries are my favorite food. I wrote a poem about them once."

That was the most she'd said since they left home. Much of the time, Charli had been able to pretend Sophia wasn't even there.

"You wrote a poem?" Rona said encouragingly. "I'd love to read it."

Sophia looked down at her hands, as if she was sorry she'd spoken. "It wasn't any good," she said. "I don't have it anymore."

"That's too bad," Ray said. "I'm impressed. I've never written a poem in my life."

"Can't you remember it, Sophia?" Rona coaxed. "We'd like to hear it."

Not me, Charli thought.

"I don't remember it," Sophia said sharply. Her cheeks were pink. "I don't know why I even mentioned it. It got burned up with some of my other stuff."

Ray put down the menu. "Burned up?" he repeated. "Do you mean *you* burned it?"

Sophia shook her head. "It was in my locker," she said in a low voice. "When my school burned."

"A school in Madison burned?" Ray asked. "When was that? I don't remember reading about it."

"Not in Madison," Sophia mumbled. "In Sacramento. Before I came to live with my great-grandmother." By now, she looked so miserable that Charli almost, but not quite, felt sorry for her.

"Oh, that must have been terrible!" Rona exclaimed. "Did you lose a lot of your things?"

"Most of my stuff was at home." Sophia stood

up then, so suddenly that she almost tipped the glass-and-wrought-iron table. "I have to go to the bathroom," she said and hurried off toward the back of the restaurant, leaving them to stare after her.

"Well," Ray murmured, "I wonder what that's all about."

"I should go after her," Charli's mother said. "She looked as if she might be sick. Or maybe she'd rather be alone. What do you think?"

The waitress arrived then with the chocolate malt and the strawberry sundae, as well as peach pie for Ray and coffee for Rona.

Charli concentrated on her malt. "She doesn't want to talk about her school burning down," she said between sips. "She doesn't want to talk about anything. Like there was a big mystery or something."

"Oh, lay off, Charli," Ray said. "There's no mystery about Sophia. She's a shy person trying to fit into a new situation. And I have a feeling you're not making it any easier for her."

Charli felt the afternoon crash in ruins around her, in spite of the malt.

"It's not my fault if she doesn't want to be friends," she said. "She doesn't like me."

Ray frowned. "Charli—" But before he could start scolding again, Rona shushed him. A moment later Sophia slid into her chair without speaking.

"Are you all right?" Rona asked. "Did we upset you, Sophia? I'm really sorry."

Sophia looked at her sundae. "I'm okay. I'm not hungry though. I thought I was, but I'm not."

"Well, take your time," Ray said. "We're in no rush. Or forget the sundae if you want. It's okay."

"I can eat it for you," Charli offered. "I don't mind."

Sophia pushed the sundae across the table. "Take it," she said. "I don't want it."

Her tone was cool and blunt, a little rude. Charli saw Ray and her mom exchange glances in the silent message-sending way grown-ups had. Now they were seeing for themselves how weird Sophia could be.

"We still have a little more shopping to do," Rona announced, after a pause. "Charli, you need a new bathing suit before you and Ray start those swimming lessons. And there's something special Sophia needs, too."

Charli put down her spoon. The reason she

needed a new swimming suit was because she'd put on weight. Yet here she was, eating a strawberry sundae after finishing every drop of her chocolate malt. She started to say she wasn't sure she wanted to learn to swim *this* summer, but Sophia spoke first.

"I don't need anything," she said, in the same cool voice she'd used before. "And I don't have any money."

"This is going to be a present, Sophia," Ray told her. "It's my idea—a sport I think you'll like. If I'm wrong, you can say so, but I'd like you to try it."

"You already bought me a present," Sophia protested. "The sweater."

"This is different."

What sport could he be talking about? Charli wondered. Whatever it was, she supposed Sophia would be good at it, the way she was good at everything else.

She picked up the spoon and swirled sweet strawberry juice into the melting ice cream. Might as well eat it, she decided. Maybe the new bathing suit would work a miracle.

Chapter Fifteen

SOPHIA'S JOURNAL

❦

I felt really stupid showing Lilly the running shoes Ray and Rona bought me. Running shoes! Why would I want to run? I told them I didn't need them and they were way too expensive, but they wouldn't listen.

Ray kept saying, "Don't say no till you try it, Sophia. . . . Lots of my students run, even if they don't take track. . . . It's good exercise . . . a great way to let off steam."

That last part worried me. There are times when I'm so uptight about what might happen next that I can hardly breathe, but I didn't think anyone had noticed.

I hoped Lilly would think the shoes were an odd gift, but instead she said, "Oh, good, Sophia! I was on the track team when I was in high school, and I loved it. I always felt so much better after a run." I knew then that she and the Franzes must have planned the shoes together. So I haven't fooled anybody. They're all watching.

I wanted to push the shoes to the back of my closet and leave them there, but of course Ray had given me all kinds of directions. Go out early in the morning. Walk at first. When you start running, don't push too hard. Rest when you get tired. You'll be surprised. . . .

If I didn't at least try it, he and Rona and Lilly would decide that, besides being strange, I was ungrateful.

I tried to be real quiet the first morning, tiptoeing down the stairs and opening the front door just partway, because it squeaks. The birds were awake, of course, and making such a racket you'd think they'd never seen the sun come up before. Lincoln Street looked peaceful in the pale light, like a movie set waiting for the actors.

I walked for a block, ran a little, and walked some more. After forty-five minutes, I was ready to go back to bed. Big deal! I thought. What's so great about this?

Yet there were some things I liked about it, even then. I didn't have to talk to anyone while I was running. I didn't even have to think! After the first couple of days, getting up early got easier and—surprise!—I decided I liked running. Sure, it's hard work at first, but then it isn't. When I went out this morning, I felt as if I had springs in my shoes.

Last night I told Lilly I was starting to enjoy it, and she was glad. No "I told you so," nothing like that. She's a good person, and so are Ray and Rona Franz.

It still bothers me, though, that they all think I have to "let off steam."

Charli was waiting in the backyard after breakfast this morning, and we cut across the field to the Castle together. She's waited there every day this week, and it's not because she loves my company. Today she wanted me to promise if that boy Jake came back, we wouldn't let him in.

"He won't be back," I said. "He didn't like us very much, remember?"

She gave me that stubborn look. "He might come," she said. "He might want to look for that woman again. The one in the living room."

I told her there hadn't been any woman in the living room, but the closer we got to the Castle, the more jittery she was. One thing's sure, I'm not the only uptight kid living on Lincoln Street.

Will's truck was in front of the house, and when we went inside we could hear him banging away in the basement.

"Don't come down here," he yelled (as if we wanted to!). "A pipe rusted out and there's two inches of water on the floor. You kids get started on the first-floor windows. Just the insides—I don't want you up on the ladder."

Good! I thought. I'd been wondering what would happen when we got around to the windows. I'd climbed a tall ladder a couple of weeks ago, but that didn't mean I wanted to do it again.

Will had mixed vinegar and water in the two buckets, and there was a pile of rags waiting on the kitchen table. We picked up what we needed and went down the hall to the living room.

"We could surprise Uncle Will and do the out-sides, too," Charli said. She had stopped near the front door, and I could tell she was just itching to go through it. "I don't mind climbing ladders."

"He doesn't want you to," I told her. "He can reach the corners easier than you can."

She didn't argue, but you could see how scared she was. The sun was shining and the living room was empty except for the chair, but she looked as if she was walking into a cave full of snakes.

I let her take the window closest to the door, and I started at the other end. She watched me at first—I don't think she'd ever washed windows before—but mostly she looked at the chair. She kept peeking over her shoulder at the wall across from the windows, too—I don't know why.

"That quilt on the chair used to be in a bedroom upstairs," she said all of a sudden. "How do you think it got down here?"

Is that all that's bothering her? I wondered. "Maybe Will brought it down to cover stains in the chair," I said. It sounded possible to me, but she shook her head.

"I hate this house," she said, glaring at the chair as if it were a wild animal that might attack at any minute. "I really hate it!"

For once I was ready to agree with her, but I managed to keep still. She's thinking about ghosts, and I've never seen anything ghostly, here or anywhere else. I don't want her telling Rona and Ray that Sophia's as scared of ghosts as she is!

I concentrated on the windows, which were really dirty. The windows in my great-grandmother's apartment never had a chance to get dirty—she washed them every single Saturday. Once, when I could tell she was feeling sick, I offered to do them for her, and she let me. When I finished, they looked exactly the way they had when I started.

Washing the Castle windows was a lot more satisfying. As I wiped away the dust, it was like lifting a curtain. The sky got bluer, and the grass across the street looked greener. I picked out Jake in the bunch of kids playing kickball in the street, and I could see chickadees fluttering around a feeder between two of the little houses.

At least, I could for a while. Then the light began to change. Oh, I could still see the birds and the kids all right, but not as clearly. And the sky was gray blue, then all gray. The view began to fade as if the sun was setting—at ten o'clock in the morning.

Charli said something, or maybe it was just a groan. I supposed she was seeing the same thing I was. "Storm's coming," I said, but I thought there had to be some other reason for the darkness. The trees weren't blowing. The kids in the street didn't stop playing to look up at the sky. The darkness came from inside the house, or inside our heads. It was as if a blanket had dropped over the Castle.

I stepped backward and bumped into the bucket, sloshing water across the floor. If Charli heard, she didn't even look in my direction. I could just make her out, standing like a statue in front of the window. I said, "Hey, are you okay?" I started toward her, and it was like walking through curtains of cob-webs. That, and the way she stood there, so still, scared me worse than the darkness.

When I was almost next to her, she whispered, "Go away—go away!" It made me mad for a second or two, until I realized she wasn't talking to me. She was talking to the window!

Chapter Sixteen
CHARLI

ꙮ

Charli stared at the *thing* in the window. It was a dark, shifting shape, about her own height, partly hidden by swirls of fog. And it was coming closer. There was no face, but when the shape flattened itself against the glass, she could feel its rage. The washrag slipped from her fingers as she ran.

Outside, the sun shone on Barker Street. The sky was a brilliant blue, without a trace of menacing gray. Charli darted through the ball game, ignoring the players, and kept going. She didn't slow down until she reached the front door of her bright blue house.

She pushed her key into the lock with trembling fingers and stumbled inside. No one was home, and the deadbolt on the door wasn't enough to make her feel safe. She ran down the hall to the bathroom and locked that door behind her, too.

Sunlight streamed through the window, filling the bathroom with warmth. She took deep breaths and looked around, grateful for familiar sights: her toothbrush in its rack, her mother's silver comb, the big bottle of bubble bath they had bought on sale at the drugstore. Ray's blue bathrobe hung behind the door.

Surely that thing, whatever it had been, couldn't follow her here. Still, the memory of the terrifying figure in the glass loomed so vividly in her head she thought she might be sick.

How could Uncle Will imagine guests would want to stay in a haunted house? If they tried it once, they would never come back. And they would tell all their friends to stay away—she had to make him believe that. Maybe her mother and Ray could help her convince him. . . .

No, not Ray. He hadn't listened before, when she tried to describe what she and Dan had heard upstairs in the Castle. Why would he listen now? He'd get angry. He'd be disappointed in her. Just when things were beginning to get better between them!

Think about that, she told herself. Think about the three afternoons this week when she and Ray had ridden their bikes to the lake as soon as he got home from work. The swimming lessons had turned out to be more fun than she'd expected. First she'd practiced floating on her back, not just for seconds but for long minutes, until she'd learned to relax and trust the water to hold her up. Then she started on a simple stroke, trying to move her arms and legs and lift her head out of the water in a steady rhythm.

It was hard work, but gradually she had begun to enjoy herself. She was a big nothing in sports at school, but with Ray's help swimming might be different. She could actually feel herself getting good at it. After the third lesson, Ray had told her she was a natural—a star pupil.

So how could the star pupil say she believed in ghosts and had seen one and never wanted to go near Crandalls' Castle again? For the first time she wondered about Sophia, who had been there when the ghost appeared. Had she seen it, too? If she had, maybe she would tell Ray. He might believe *her*.

She stood up and looked at herself in the mirror above the sink. Her face was splotchy and her hair was limp with sweat. She felt hot but shivery at the same time.

"I really am sick," she told the mirror. "I'm too sick to work."

Being sick meant chicken soup and crackers in bed, instead of pork chops and mashed potatoes in the kitchen. It meant having your temperature taken and swallowing two oversized vitamin C capsules. It meant milk and buttered toast for breakfast instead of waffles with syrup, and, since she had finished all this week's library books, it meant being stuck with nothing new to read.

On the good side, it meant that her mother and Ray fussed over her, stopping at her bedroom door often to ask how she was feeling. It meant a whole plate of Aunt Lilly's chocolate chip cookies, in case she began to recover. Being sick meant having Uncle Will sit on the edge of the bed and tell her funny stories. It even meant having Sophia come to visit. She and Lilly appeared the next afternoon with flowers from the Crandalls' backyard and a dish of cinnamon-flavored custard.

"I can't stay," Aunt Lilly said. "I left the boys out on your porch, because Gene has the sniffles. We don't want to add a cold to your problems, dear." She gave Charli a kiss on the top of her head and hurried out, leaving the two girls in an uncomfortable silence.

"Sorry you're sick," Sophia said, finally. "You should have said something yesterday."

So that was how it was going to be. If she'd seen anything frightening at the Castle, she wasn't going to say so.

"I felt funny," Charli mumbled. "You know, like I might faint. Everything was getting dark so I . . . Did you stay all morning? Did you see how dark it got?"

Sophia ignored the last question. "I told Will you'd left, and he said I should go, too. The leak in the pipe is much worse than he thought, and he's going to have to talk to a man at the hardware store about how to fix it. Or maybe get a plumber. He thinks all the pipes might have to be replaced."

"That's awful!" Charli exclaimed. "That would cost a ton of money." She thought of Uncle Will, trying to make her feel better last night and keeping this big worry to himself.

"Will said to give you this," Sophia said. "He said you wanted something to read."

Charli groaned. The book was the autobiography of William Herndon that Uncle Will had been carrying around in his truck.

"I'd rather read about kings and queens and movie stars." She hesitated, feeling childish again under Sophia's cool gaze. "Have you read it?"

Sophia shook her head. "Not yet. I forgot about it."

"You can have it first," Charli offered, but Sophia was already starting for the door.

"Maybe later," she said over her shoulder. "I'm going to take care of the kids this afternoon while Lilly makes new curtains for the catchall room."

"You mean your bedroom," Charli said, but Sophia had already gone.

The book was called *The Story of a Life*. Couldn't William Herndon have thought up a more exciting title? Charli thought, bored already. If he was smart enough to become governor, he should have been able to do better than that. Yawning, she opened the book to the first page.

My life almost ended soon after it began.

She sat up straighter, startled by this unexpected first sentence.

To the eyes of others, I must have seemed a most fortunate child, and in many ways I was. My father was wealthy, and we lived in the largest house in the town of Mount Pleasant, Wisconsin. But there was a dangerous situation in our household of which my parents were unaware. My mother's younger sister Jennifer had moved in with them after she was left an orphan. She imagined herself in love with my father. He had courted her briefly before asking Dorothy, my mother, to marry him.

The three lived together in outward peace for two years, without any indication that my aunt was jealous, bitterly resentful, and becoming increasingly unstable. She believed people gossiped about her and pitied her, and perhaps she was right. Small towns can be cruel. Perhaps she dreamed that one day my father would realize he had married the wrong sister. After I was born, however, that secret hope died. According to all accounts, my mother and father were happier and more in love than ever.

When I was two years old, my parents invited friends for a Fourth of July picnic in our backyard, followed by fireworks. Nobody noticed Jennifer slip away as the fireworks began. I was upstairs asleep, but fortunately my mother decided to carry me outside to see the bright colors. When she reached the nursery, she saw an incredible sight. Jennifer was holding something—a pillow or a blanket—over my face. If my mother hadn't arrived when she did, I would certainly have suffocated. Jennifer shrieked in rage and attacked my mother viciously. She never spoke a sane word again.

I didn't hear this story until I was in my teens, and even then my mother couldn't tell it without crying. For nearly a year Jennifer was confined to a back bedroom, with nurses to care for her day and night. My mother said they could hear her sobbing for hours at a time, and, chillingly, she often begged to have the "dear baby" brought to her so she could hold it. When she died, it must have been a relief to everyone.

"We didn't dare let her near you," my mother told me with tears in her eyes.

Soon after Jennifer's death, my parents, eager to escape painful memories, sold the house and moved to Appleton, where I grew up and they lived to celebrate their fifty-fifth wedding anniversary.

Charli couldn't eat the soup her mother brought in for supper, and she turned down Ray's offer to drive into town for ice cream.

"Maybe you should see the doctor," Rona said anxiously. "It scares me when you turn down ice cream, Charli. What are we going to do with you?"

"I'll be okay," Charli said.

"Sure you will," Ray agreed. "You'll be fine."

She could tell by the way he looked at her that he had begun to suspect she wasn't really sick. But he's wrong, she thought miserably. If she'd been halfway pretending before, she wasn't now. Her head throbbed and her stomach churned every time she thought about the madwoman who had tried to kill little William Herndon and had died in a back bedroom of the Castle.

Chapter Seventeen
SOPHIA'S JOURNAL

Today started off well enough—very well, actually. The twins and Mickey and I went to the beach, which is something I wouldn't have thought of doing a few weeks ago. I know the kids now, and they know me. Terry is the twin who thinks up exciting things to do, and Gene is the one who does them—and gets into trouble. If you keep Terry busy and safe, Gene will be okay. Today they decided to build a whole city of sand—houses and walls, even a park.

Mickey and I gathered twigs to make trees in the park. Mickey is the best little kid in the world, always smiling and just thrilled when his brothers don't shoo him away from what they're doing. If I ever have a baby, I want him to be just like Mickey.

When we went home about three-thirty, Charli was sitting on the Franzes' front steps with Lilly. Lilly called, "Look! Charli's feeling better! I made her come out to soak up some sun." Then she pointed up at my bedroom windows so I would see the new curtains.

I crossed the street, thinking I'd sit with them for a while, but I could feel Charli hoping I wouldn't. So I plopped Mickey on the grass in front of them and left Terry and Gene to brag about all their good work at the beach.

The curtains are beautiful. Lilly made them from a bedsheet and added wide blue ribbon tie-backs, the same shade as the blue in her mother's quilt. I sat on the bed and admired them, and then I put on my running shoes. A good long run sounded like the right end to the day.

I slipped out the back door and through the trees at the end of the yard, then along the field to the curve where Lincoln Street turns into a gravel road. There was no one else around as I started to run, and when I reached Barker Street, it was empty, too. Will's truck and a plumber's van were in front of the Castle, but the kids who usually hang out in the street weren't there today.

I ran one more block and then turned toward the lake road, where I'd walked with the boys earlier. The sun was bright, and the breeze off the lake was just starting to turn cool. I just about flew! It was perfect—that moment at the top of the roller coaster ride just before the car starts hurtling down.

At the end of the beach there's a sort of breakwater made of boulders and big chunks of concrete. I slowed down and looked out over the lake. It was ridged with tiny glittering ripples, and there was a row of sailboats bobbing along like toys. I sat on a rock, thinking about nothing except how lucky I was to be there. And then, so quickly I couldn't believe it, the happy feeling began to fade. The lake was still there, and the sun and the boats, but I wasn't. I was in St. Joseph's Hospital in Madison. I saw green walls and the high, white bed, and I saw my great-grandmother lying gray-faced and still. She looked almost the way she'd looked the last time I saw her—but different, too. I closed my eyes and waited. When I opened them, I was back on the breakwater, with the lake and the sand and the sun. A gull landed a few feet away. He must have thought I'd stopped for lunch, because he walked stiff-legged in front of me, searching for crumbs.

I slid off the rock and started to run back the

way I'd come. All I could think of was that I had to get home to the Crandalls as fast as possible. I wanted their talk and their jokes and their crazy games to crowd out what I'd just seen. I wanted to hug Mickey and hear him laugh. I imagined the kitchen full of late-afternoon light and good smells, with Lilly at the stove and the baby in his high chair.

I was concentrating so hard that I almost bumped into Charli halfway up the beach. She was at the edge of the road, just standing there, and when I got close enough I could see her eyes were red, as if she'd been crying.

"Lilly sent me," she said. "She wants you to come home right away."

"That's what I'm doing," I snapped. I really hated her right then—she doesn't have a clue how lucky she is. "Why are you crying?" I said, mean as poison. "It's not *your* great-grandmother who's dead."

As soon as the words were out, I knew what I'd done, but it was too late. Her eyes got huge behind her glasses.

"How'd you know?" she asked. "Somebody just called Lilly from Madison a few minutes ago. How'd you know?"

I didn't answer. I couldn't. We stared at each

other for what seemed like a long time, and finally she said, "Go ahead and run if you want to."

I ran, glad to get away. When I turned off the lake road I glanced back and she was still standing there, staring out at the water. Probably wondering whom she should tell first about weird Sophia.

Chapter Eighteen
SOPHIA'S JOURNAL

Lilly was on the phone making plans when I got back to the house. She threw her arms around me and told me how sorry she was about my loss. Then she said she realized I'd want to go to the funeral, and I didn't have to worry because she and I would go to Madison together.

"Charli can come with us if she wants to," she said. "It would do her good to get away for a day. I just talked to Mary Kramer down the street, and she'll watch the boys while Dan is at work."

That was two days ago, and until we left this morning I kept trying to get up the nerve to tell her I didn't want to go. What's the point? My great-grandmother won't know I'm there, and if she did know she wouldn't care. I was just a stranger she'd had to look out for.

In the end I didn't say it, because Lilly is my ideal person. She's kind and good and she loves everyone. If she knew what I'm like inside, she'd be shocked.

The Franzes let us take their car so we wouldn't have to take the bus to Madison. I hoped Charli would stay home, but no luck. When we went outside, there she was, sitting cross-legged in the backseat, waiting. I said hi, but I didn't look at her. I was sure she was waiting for a chance to ask again how I knew my great-grandmother was dead before anyone told me.

It's a good thing Lilly likes to talk—I don't think she even noticed how quiet her passengers were. She talked about the weather and Dan's job and how hard Will was working at the Castle, and how the twins were growing so fast she'd have to buy them new clothes to start kindergarten. She didn't mention the funeral once, so there were minutes at a time when I could pretend this was just a little holiday trip on a pretty summer day. Then I'd feel Charli's eyes boring into the back of my head, and it stopped being a holiday.

I'd never been to a funeral before, not even my

mom's. I guess whoever was taking care of me then decided I was too young. My great-grandmother's service was in a big old funeral home that smelled of disinfectant. We sat in a row, Lilly and Charli and me, in front of the closed-up casket, while an organ played in another room and the funeral director read from the Bible and said some prayers. Lilly squeezed my hand and wiped her eyes once or twice, and I felt bad because I didn't feel bad, if you know what I mean. I know my great-grandmother couldn't help the way she was, but I can't pretend I'll miss her. Not even to satisfy Lilly.

When the service was over, I turned around and there—sitting right behind us—was Rita, the social worker from St. Joseph's Hospital. That scared me! Until that moment it hadn't occurred to me that my great-grandmother's death would make a difference in whether I stayed or didn't stay with the Crandalls. But when I saw Rita, I knew it made a *big* difference. Social workers have rules for everything. She had asked Lilly if I could stay in Mount Pleasant while my great-grandmother was in the hospital. Now that she's dead, I'll have to go back to Sacramento.

Rita patted my shoulder and asked how I was, but she didn't fool me. It was Lilly she'd come to see. She said, "You girls must be tired of sitting—

why don't you take a little walk while we chat?" As if we were Gene and Terry's age.

I wanted to stay right there to hear every word they said, but Lilly looked so worried and sad, I didn't argue. Her cheerful chatter on the way to Madison had been a big cover-up for the bad news she knew was coming.

The heat was fierce when we stepped out onto the wide front porch of the funeral home. I started down the steps but Charli stopped me.

"It's too hot," she said. She pointed to a swing at the far end of the porch. "Let's sit. I have to ask you something."

Well, here it comes, I thought. And then I realized it didn't matter now—let her ask. Rita was in there telling Lilly what was what, and nothing Charli told them about me was going to make any difference.

"I knew my great-grandmother was dead because I saw her," I said flat out, hoping to shock her. "I saw her in her hospital room and I looked at her and I knew. It happens to me that way sometimes, like a dream, only I'm awake and what I see is real."

She stared at me. "Is that the truth?"

"Of course it's the truth," I said. "How else could I have known?"

She said, "You might have guessed. That's what I thought. I thought you were worried about your great-grandmother, and so you just guessed. Anyway," she went on, "that isn't what I want to ask. Tell me what you saw in the Castle Friday morning—just before I went home."

Went home? I thought. Ha! That was a pretty funny way to describe how she'd dashed out of the house.

"The living room got dark," I said. "It was dark outside, too. I thought a storm was coming, but it never happened. Period."

She looked disappointed. "Is that all? Didn't you see anything—a person—reflected in the glass?"

I shook my head. "No ghost, if that's what you mean. People only see ghosts if they want to believe they are there. You believe so—"

"Then I suppose you think the Castle's a really neat place," she said angrily. "I suppose you think millions of people are going to want to stay there."

I tried to find a way to answer without saying too much. "Well, I wouldn't stay there myself," I said. "I think there's something wrong, but I don't know what."

Her eyes narrowed. "Do you think it the way you thought your great-grandmother was dead?"

"Sort of."

Her anger melted. "Okay then," she said. "That's good. You can tell Uncle Will and my folks that we shouldn't work there anymore. Tell them William Herndon's aunt went crazy in the Castle when he was a baby and tried to suffocate him! She's still hanging around there, and we can prove it. Dan and I heard a woman singing and a baby crying upstairs even though now he won't admit it happened. And before that I saw the shadow of a cradle in the living room. And you were there this week when everything went dark, even if you didn't see the—see Jennifer—in the window. Tell them it's a horrible house with an awful ghost wandering around looking for the baby she tried to kill!"

She had it all figured out, and if everything she said was true, she might even be right. Still, I didn't want any part in it.

"Let's tell Uncle Will together," she coaxed. "I'll be there, but you talk. He thinks you're really smart. So does Ray—they think I'm faking and being silly, but they'll believe you."

I said, "They won't believe me, because I'm not going to tell them any of that. I've never seen a ghost, so just leave me out of it, okay?"

I felt like such a rat. I knew how scared she was.

She'd hoped I would help, and instead I was making her feel worse—more alone—than ever.

It was a relief when the door of the funeral home opened and Lilly and Rita came out onto the porch—a relief, except that they both looked grim.

Chapter Nineteen
CHARLI

"Nobody can tell him anything," Ray said. "Once the guy gets an idea in his head he's stubborn as a mule. Now he thinks the bank will lend him enough money to replace all the plumbing in that old wreck."

Charli followed the voice to the kitchen. Uncle Will again, she thought tiredly. She'd been thinking a lot about Uncle Will on the way back from Madison and had begun to realize some-thing painful. Even though she loved him a lot, there were times when she didn't like him much. Right now, for instance, she didn't mind Ray saying he was as stubborn as a mule.

"Charli!" Her mother's smile was as warm as a hug. "How did the day go? How is Sophia?

I've been thinking about you and Aunt Lilly all day. Was the funeral very sad?"

"Sort of." Charli pictured the dreary room in the funeral home with its rows of empty folding chairs. "Aunt Lilly cried."

"Your Aunt Lilly is a rare bird," Ray said. "She feels sorry for everyone but herself. How about Sophia?"

Charli shrugged. "She's all right, I guess. Nobody talked on the way home."

Her mother and Ray looked at each other. "Was anyone else at the funeral?" Rona asked.

"A lady," Charli said. "She and Aunt Lilly talked for a while."

Another meaningful glance.

Her mother set the salad bowl and a basket of rolls on the table. Then she sat down and reached for Charli's hand and Ray's. "This is so nice," she said, "the three of us together. It's good to be able to talk things over at the end of the day." She squeezed Charli's hand and Charli squeezed back.

"I just hope your appetite has come back," Rona said. "You still look pretty pale, hon."

"I'm okay," Charli said. "Aunt Lilly bought ice-cream cones on the way home so . . ."

She let the words trail off, aware that Ray was watching her as he buttered a roll. "Dan and the kids were here a while ago," he said with a grin. "He had some news that's going to make you feel better, I think. The water's been turned off at the Castle, so you and Sophia won't be able to work there for a few days. Too bad, huh?"

Charli took a deep breath. With each passing mile of the trip home she had become more confused about what she would do next. Sophia had been her only hope, and she'd refused to help. That meant Charli had three choices, all bad. She could go on pretending to be too sick to work. She could tell her mother and Ray about the ghost and hope they would believe her. Or—and this was the worst—she could go back to work in the Castle.

Now she wouldn't have to do any of those things. How long would it take for a plumber to fix what was wrong at the Castle? A long time, she hoped. A long, long time!

"Well, come on," Ray teased, "how does it feel to know you can spend the day lying under a tree reading again?"

"You think I'm lazy," Charli said, but she was much too relieved to be angry. "I can do chores around here," she said. "And I can go swimming."

"Both good ideas," Ray said. "Only you don't go swimming alone. It's not safe."

"Ask Sophia," Rona suggested. "She'll be looking for things to do, too—for a while anyway."

Charli nodded, but she knew she wouldn't ask Sophia. She wouldn't ask her for anything ever again. Sophia tried to be mysterious with her talk about knowing things before they happened, but the truth was, Sophia was a snob. She definitely didn't want to be Charli's friend.

"How about some salad?" Ray asked, pushing the bowl across the table. "Your mom's a terrific salad-maker."

Charli speared two slices of ham from the platter and took a big helping of salad.

"Well, thank goodness," Rona said, and she and Ray looked at each other again.

They were laughing at her full plate, but Charli didn't mind. Tomorrow she would clean the whole house to show Ray she wasn't lazy, but all she could think about now was how good the food tasted. "What's for dessert?" she asked, so she could look forward to it. "I'm starving."

*　　　*　　　*

It was going to be a neat day. No Castle, nothing to be afraid of, just hours and hours to use however she pleased. Charli stretched, yawned, and pressed her cheek into her pillow where the morning sun had warmed it. Uncle Will had crossed the street last night to tell her himself that he wouldn't need her and Sophia for a while. A plumber was coming to the Castle today to decide what needed to be done. It would be at least a week before he could get started.

"We'll just have ourselves a little vacation," Uncle Will said. "You kids won't mind that, I bet. And it'll give me some time to talk to the bank—maybe round up a few folks around town who know a good investment when they see one."

Charli tried not to look pleased. "Mom and Ray are in the backyard if you want to talk to them," she said, but Uncle Will just tousled her hair.

"Not right now," he said. "I've got some paperwork to do."

There was something different about his walk, Charli thought as she watched him cross the street. His thin shoulders were hunched, and he walked more slowly than usual. She was glad Ray hadn't been there to laugh at what he'd said about rounding up folks who knew a good investment when they saw one.

So what should she do with this lovely, empty day? The library first, she decided. As soon as her mother and Ray left for work, she got her bike from the garage and swung out onto Lincoln. From across the street came the sound of Aunt Lilly's laughter and the twins squabbling. The familiar voices made her feel lonely and left out, but only for a moment. Then she pushed the feelings away and pedaled faster.

When she returned an hour and a half later, her bike basket was stacked with three mysteries, a collection of short stories for teens, and a true tale of dogsled racing in Alaska. Enough for a week, she thought contentedly, as she parked her bike and headed for her favorite spot under the crab apple tree.

The first mystery was so exciting that she almost, but not quite, forgot about lunch. Still reading, she ambled into the house to make a sandwich and check the cookie jar. Have to do some chores, she reminded herself. Just a few more pages . . .

It was after three when she finished the last chapter. Ray would be home in a few minutes— not enough time even to wash the kitchen floor or clean the bathroom. There had to be something else she could do, something he would surely notice.

The living room was a mess, with his favorite magazines scattered around his chair and even behind it. She scooped them up and arranged them in two neat piles on the coffee table. Then she straightened the towels in the bathroom, put her lunch dishes in the dishwasher, and was giving the counter a quick wipe when the front door opened. Just in time, she thought, but it was Dan, not Ray, who appeared in the hallway.

"Hey," he exclaimed in mock surprise. "Do you still live here? Could have fooled me."

"I was sick," Charli said, not quite meeting his eyes. "And I went to Madison. Why aren't you at work?"

"Early shift," Dan said. "Right now I'm working at home—monster-sitting." He glanced over his shoulder, and Charli heard the twins making engine noises across the street. "Mom's at the dentist and Dad's off trying to raise money"—he scowled—"and Sophia's on one of her long-distance runs. So that leaves me. There's a pan of fudge in our kitchen. Interested?" He grinned as Charli dropped the dishcloth.

The sky had turned gray and a breeze sifted

through the trees that lined the street. Make-believe motors roaring, Terry and Gene pushed toy cars across the lawn in front of their house while Mickey cheered from his stroller.

"Give the fudge a few more minutes to cool," Dan said when they reached the porch steps. "Sophia made it before she took off. Why can't you make great stuff like that?"

"I could," Charli retorted. "If I wanted to!" She knew she should ignore his teasing, but she couldn't resist letting him know she was good at something, too. "I'm the only one who's figured out who the ghost in the Castle is. Not Sophia. Just me."

Dan groaned. "Don't start that again."

"I'm not starting anything!" Charli raised her voice above the *zoom zoom* of the twins' cars. "I'm just telling you." Quickly, before he could interrupt, she explained what she'd learned from William Herndon's autobiography. "And besides that, I saw the ghost myself. In a window," she finished. "It—she was horrible!"

She stopped, out of breath, and waited for Dan to tell her she was crazy.

"Okay, so you have it all figured out," he said. "Big deal! What difference does it make? Nobody's going to take you seriously, except maybe my dad, because he'd like there to be a ghost."

"My mom and Ray might believe it if you told them what we heard upstairs—that singing and the baby crying. Then they wouldn't make me work there anymore." She looked at Dan hopefully, but, as she'd feared, he shook his head.

"Someone was playing a trick on us that day, kid. I don't know who or why, but it had to be a trick. So don't ask me to get mixed up in your scary daydreams. Ray would think I was nuts, and I wouldn't blame him. Get a life, Charli. Find something else to think about. How are the swimming lessons?"

"Good," Charli said shortly. Her face burned. He was treating her like a baby again. Why wouldn't anyone listen?

"Here comes Mom." Dan stood up, looking relieved. "That means I'm off duty as a sitter. Want to go in and check that fudge?"

Charli waved at Aunt Lilly, who had just appeared at the end of the block, and followed Dan inside. The Crandalls' kitchen, once her favorite place in the world, looked unfamiliar. It had been a long time since she'd stopped in to sample whatever had just come out of the oven.

"Help yourself," Dan said. "I'm going to check the voice mail." He sprawled at the table with the phone clamped to his ear and a faraway look in his eyes.

Charli searched a drawer for a knife and reached for the pan of fudge. It looked delicious. It *was* delicious. Perfect Sophia had done it again! She was finishing a second piece and considering a third when Dan finally put down the phone and grabbed a pencil and notepad. He wrote busily for a moment, then took the piece of fudge she passed him.

"I cut some for the twins," Charli said, so he wouldn't notice how much she'd eaten herself. "Can Mickey have a little piece, too?"

"Ask Mom," Dan said absentmindedly. He was staring at the note he'd just written, as if it puzzled him. Then he gave Charli a startled look. "Hey, it's awfully quiet out there," he said. "I wonder—"

Abruptly, he pushed back his chair, almost knocking it over in his rush to the front door. Charli hurried after him, licking crumbs from her fingers.

"They're gone!" Dan exclaimed. "All three of them. Now where in the heck!" He dashed out into the street.

Charli stared at the bright-colored cars scattered like flowers on the grass. "Maybe they're in the backyard," she suggested, but she knew they couldn't be. The kitchen windows were open. She would have heard the boys if they were playing back there.

"They can't be far," she hurried on, because the look on Dan's face was painful to see. "Maybe they took Mickey down the block to meet Aunt Lilly and she stopped at somebody's house and—they're okay."

"Yeah, sure," Dan said in a tight voice. "They're okay." He started to run.

Chapter Twenty

SOPHIA'S JOURNAL

❧❦❧

It's five-thirty, but Lilly said forget about dinner till Will comes home, and she said it in such a sad, un-Lilly-like voice that I wanted to be somewhere else. So here I am, talking to you, because if ever I needed to talk it's now. When I tell you about today, you're going to think, oh, that never happened. But it did.

Breakfast this morning was pretty grim, mostly because Lilly was so quiet. Usually she rattles on like a kid, but not today. At first I thought she was just tired after the drive to Madison, but then I caught her looking at me a couple of times and turning away, fast, when I looked back. Boy, do I know that expression! Good old Rita must have given her the job of telling me I have to go back to Sacramento.

I wondered if I should bring up the subject myself, so she could stop worrying, but I couldn't make myself do it. Instead, I took Mickey for a long ride in his stroller. I wanted to get out of the house, and besides, it might be my last chance to spend some time alone with him. He calls me So-ee now, and he listens when I tell him things. Today I promised I'd never forget him, and I might return someday to see what kind of man he turns out to be.

When we got back to the house, I made peanut-butter-and-pickle sandwiches for lunch. Lilly was getting ready to go to the dentist. She said Dan would be home early to take care of the boys, so I could do whatever I wanted to this afternoon.

"We take advantage of you, Sophia," she said. "I'm sorry." I suppose she was trying to convince both of us that I'd be happier someplace else.

As soon as Dan came home, I put on my running shoes and left. There were fat puffy clouds piling up in the west, some of them pretty dark, but I didn't care. The way I felt, I wanted a storm, with me in the middle of it.

By the time I reached the beach road the wind

had picked up, and the lake was streaked with white-caps. People were gathering up their towels and their kids, and one little girl cried because she didn't want to leave. Farther along, I saw what was left of Gene and Terry's sand city. Another few hours and it would be gone, as if it had never been there.

I passed the breakwater, the place where I'd learned my great-grandmother was dead. Beyond, the summer cottages were strung along the shore like toy houses, each with its own plot of trees and straggly lawn. A few kids spilled out onto the road, and some of them ran beside me for a minute or two. I slowed down so they could keep up.

I'm telling you all this little stuff because I want you to see how ordinary it was and how unprepared I was for what came next.

The kids dropped back, giggling, so that by the time I rounded the next curve, I was alone again. What I saw then, as clearly as I'd seen the cottages behind me, was the Crandalls' gray house. It was a couple of hundred feet away and directly ahead, so that the road I was on ended at the porch steps.

I stopped. I knew the house wasn't really there, but I wasn't scared, not at first. It looked so peaceful—toys on the steps and on the porch, the screen door hanging open because the spring was shot—all just as I'd left it. Except, it was quiet.

Too quiet.

I told myself the twins and Mickey could have gone away with Dan—maybe across the street to Charli's house—but I didn't believe it. Suddenly I was terrified. The house had appeared because something awful was happening. It was the awful thing I'd sensed that night I met the Crandalls for the first time. And I hadn't tried to warn them— not then, not ever. It had always been more important to keep quiet.

All the way back to Lincoln Street I prayed, Let me be wrong. Let the kids be where I left them. But then I saw Lilly come out of Mrs. Kramer's house on the corner with Dan and Charli, and I stopped praying. If God heard what I was asking, the answer was definitely NO!

Dan said, "The kids are gone. We thought they might have walked down the block to meet Mom, but she stopped in to see—"

"Call the police, Dan!" Lilly interrupted. Her blue eyes were bigger than ever, and her face was white. "They can't be far. Unless someone picked them up . . ." Her voice shook.

"They've gone to the Castle," I said. "They can see it from your yard. Will talks about it so much they think it's a big deal—like a castle in a picture book."

"The Castle," Lilly repeated. "How can you possibly know——"

"I do know!" I yelled. "I do! That's where they're going, and we have to stop them!"

I started to run again, and after a moment I heard the others running behind me. When we reached the house (toys on the porch steps, just as I'd seen them), I cut around to the backyard. The kids would have used the road that wound around to Barker Street—no way could they push Mickey's stroller through the field. We took the shortcut.

"If that's really where they went, they won't be able to get in," Dan panted as we dashed through the trees and out into the field.

"They can," I said without slowing down. "The plumber's coming today. Will said he'd leave the door unlocked for him."

I could see it all clearly—the twins dragging Mickey's stroller up the steps, Terry opening the door, stepping inside . . .

Someone stumbled and fell behind me, and I thought, Poor Lilly, how can she run in her best shoes? Charli sobbed and Dan muttered, "This is crazy!" but we kept on going.

That was the fastest I've ever run. I felt as if I was barely touching the ground. When I came out into Barker Street, Jake was on the curb, staring at the Castle. His face was pale under a layer of grime.

"They went in there," he said, before I could ask if he'd seen two small boys pushing a baby's stroller. He pointed across the street with an expression that said you wouldn't catch *him* in there again—not ever.

"What'd he say?" Dan demanded. "Are they here?"

I nodded, and we raced across the street. We were all together again; Lilly had lost her shoes, and she and Charli ran hand in hand. Dan threw open the Castle door.

Gene and Terry must have been huddled just inside. Dan's shove sent them sprawling across the tiles, where they landed in a tangle, shrieking. When they saw Lilly, they scrambled up and buried their faces in her skirt.

I stared at the empty stroller. That was the worst moment of my entire life—up to then, that is. The very worst was still ahead.

We all yelled, "Where's Mickey?" and Lilly tried to push the twins away so they could answer. They clung to her and cried as if they'd never stop.

She grabbed Terry's shoulders and shook him. "Tell us where Mickey is, hon," she said. "Did you leave him somewhere?"

Terry didn't answer, but Gene turned around, one fist still clutching the skirt. He pointed at the stairs.

"We didn't leave him anywhere!" He sounded outraged. "We wouldn't ever! A lady took him up there. She said to wait here till she came back."

Dan and I were halfway up the stairs before he finished, and Charli was right behind us. I know I've called her a crybaby, but she's a pretty good kid after all. She'd spent the last few days trying to figure out a way to keep from ever seeing the inside of the Castle again, but there she was.

At the top of the stairs, she pointed down the hall to the right. "Down there," she said. "The last room. Remember, Dan?"

Now we could hear Mickey crying. I wanted to cry myself. His sobs sounded muffled and very far away.

"Where is he?" Lilly gasped. She was struggling up the stairs, dragging the twins behind her.

Dan reached the last door before I did and opened it.

A blast of dank, icy air hit us. Wind roared through the room, almost drowning Mickey's screams. There was another sound, too. A woman was singing "Rock-a-bye Baby" in a horrible shrill voice.

Gene and Terry burst into howls, and Lilly dragged them back, away from the door. Dan and Charli and I clung to one another—the wind was that strong—and stared at the bed in the middle of the room. The quilt—the same one that had been on the chair downstairs the last time I saw it—was on the bed, and someone was struggling beneath it. It was a small someone, kicking, crying, choking. The quilt clung to him as if it were alive.

We tried to run to the bed, but the wind was like a wall pushing us backward. Then the lullaby changed to laughter. Dan lunged forward, pulling Charli and me with him, and we all grabbed the edge of the quilt.

It was just an ordinary quilt, worn and faded, but when we pulled, it didn't move. Not one inch! It was as if steel fingers held it down over that struggling little shape.

I screamed, and Charli screamed, too. Dan yelled, "Pull"—as if we weren't! The wind knocked me to my knees, and when I stood up it pushed me sideways. I bumped into Charli and she bumped Dan, and for a second I thought we were all going over like dominoes. But we held on. Charli yelled, "Jennifer! Jennifer!" as if she could actually see who was holding down the quilt.

Then it was over. The quilt flew off the bed, and

all three of us crashed into the wall behind us. The wind and the laughter stopped. Mickey lay in the middle of the shabby mattress, limp as a doll, his eyes closed. I thought he was dead.

That was it—the very worst moment of my life. I'll never forget it, and I'm sure the others won't either. It was probably only seconds that we stood there, unable to move, but it seemed much longer until his eyelids fluttered, and he began to cry.

Dan scooped him up and handed him to Lilly, who was in the doorway. She looked as if she was going to faint, with Terry clutching one of her knees and Gene the other. Then we all crowded out into the hall. I was afraid to turn my back on that awful room and I guess Dan and Charli felt the same way. We didn't start to run until Dan slammed the door. Then I grabbed Gene and Dan picked up Terry, and we took off. Charli snatched up the stroller at the foot of the stairs, and we burst out the front door.

Jake was still there. He got an eyeful—three little boys sobbing and the rest of us looking scared out of our skulls. He'd have a lot to tell all his pals who had missed the show!

When we reached the field Dan set Gene on his feet and took the stroller from Charli. Lilly said, "Watch for my shoes," and I realized that was the first time any of us had spoken. "I don't re-member where I lost them," she said, like a tired little girl.

I wondered what she was thinking. She didn't know Charli had been convinced there were ghosts in the Castle since the first day she went inside. She hadn't heard about William Herndon's insane aunt Jennifer. She must have a million questions rattling around in her head, along with one particular one I didn't want to answer.

We got as far as the sandbox in the Crandalls' backyard. It was raining by then—just a fine mist that actually felt good. Lilly slumped on the edge of the box with Mickey, sound asleep, in her arms. The twins pressed against her on either side, and Charli and Dan and I stood in front of her.

"All right, tell me," she said. "Somebody please explain what happened back there."

I looked at Charli, and so did Dan. She was the one who had believed, and we had brushed her off. Her voice trembled as she repeated the William Herndon story and described what she and Dan had heard when they went to the Castle together.

"Why didn't you tell us all this?" Lilly asked. She didn't sound angry, just puzzled.

Charli said, "Ray doesn't believe in ghosts. He'd think I was trying to get out of work."

"But what about Uncle Will? You could have told him."

Dan answered. "I told her not to. I told her Dad would consider a ghost a—an added attraction. And you"—he sounded apologetic—"you always think he's right."

Lilly nodded. She looked down at Mickey and then at me, and at that moment Gene announced that he was hungry.

I could have hugged him. "Come on," I said, "I'll make a sandwich for you."

We were safely in the back hall when I heard the question I'd been dreading. "I don't understand any of this," Lilly said. "How did Sophia know where the boys had gone? How could she be so sure?"

I waited long enough to hear Charli answer for me. "Sophia knows stuff before it happens," she said. "She told me so."

It sounded crazy, but no crazier than the rest of what she'd been explaining. I held my breath, waiting for Lilly to say "Don't be silly, that's not possible." What she said was, "Thank God!"

Chapter Twenty-One
CHARLI

⁂

"Okay if we hang out here for a while?" Dan loomed in the kitchen doorway with Mickey on his shoulders. The twins crowded close behind him. "We just got kicked out of our house, more or less."

"Dan, shame on you!" Charli's mom hurried to fill a plate with chocolate chip cookies while Ray pulled extra chairs up to the table. "Your mother would never kick you out, no matter what awful thing you did! She has the patience of a saint."

Dan gave cookies to Gene and Terry and broke one in half for Mickey. "She'd have thrown Sophia out, too," he said, "if she weren't already hiding upstairs in her bedroom."

"Sophia hiding?" Ray frowned. "I doubt that. What's going on over there, anyway?"

Charli kept her eyes on her empty soup bowl, not wanting to meet Dan's incredulous gaze. Of course she hadn't told her folks anything, not yet. Of course she was going to do it—maybe after supper, when Ray was relaxing in his favorite chair with another cup of coffee.

"Sophia isn't in some kind of trouble, is she?" Rona asked anxiously.

Charli couldn't keep still any longer. "Sophia saved Mickey's life today, that's all!" she blurted out. "The ghost in the Castle was going to smother him, but Sophia knew where he was, and—"

"Charli," Ray interrupted sternly, "don't talk nonsense. Just tell us what happened, without the spooks!"

"She can't tell it without a spook, Ray," Dan said. "No way! There *is* a ghost in that place, and Charli's the only person who was sure of it— until today." He faltered under Ray's disgusted glare. "Ask Mom," he said. "She'll tell you. She saw the whole thing."

"Saw what whole thing?" Rona asked. "What are you talking about?"

Charli sneaked a glance at Ray. This was even

worse than she'd feared it would be. His face was red, and he looked as if he might explode. He would never believe there was a ghost, even if Aunt Lilly said it was true.

Right now he's probably wishing he'd never married us, she thought. He's wondering how he ever got mixed up with such a goofy family!

The first notes of "Yankee Doodle" sounded from the street, providing a welcome interruption. Gene and Terry raced down the hall to the front door with Dan in pursuit.

"Not yet, you guys," he called. "Mom wants to talk to Dad for a while—alone!"

Charli squirmed unhappily. When Dan didn't return, she took off her glasses and pretended to examine them.

"Hey, I need new frames," she said. "These are bent." She held them out, but her mother and Ray ignored them.

"Don't change the subject," Ray growled. "Tell us what this is about and skip the trimmings."

A low whistle came from the hall. "Will you look at that!" Dan exclaimed in a wondering voice.

Charli didn't need a second invitation. She bounded from her chair and ran to the front door.

She saw Uncle Will first. He was getting out of his truck, and he looked more rumpled than usual. Then she saw Aunt Lilly on the front porch.

But was it really Aunt Lilly? She looked taller, and her lips were pressed into a thin line. Even at this distance, Charli imagined sparks in those gentle blue eyes.

"Good grief!" Ray muttered. He and Rona had joined them at the door. "Lilly looks like Joan of Arc going into battle!"

Charli didn't know much about Joan of Arc, but she held her breath as Uncle Will climbed the porch steps. His head was down, so he didn't notice Aunt Lilly until he almost bumped into her. Then he, too, stared in astonishment.

"She's telling him something," Charli whispered. "What's she saying?" She strained to hear, but Aunt Lilly spoke softly. Softly, but not fooling around, Charli thought. No smile. No laughing. Just a steady torrent of words that seemed to hit Uncle Will like hailstones.

"She has to be telling him what happened," Dan said. "Boy is she ever telling him!"

"But what *did* happen?" Rona demanded. "Why won't you and Charli explain what your mother is so upset about?"

"We did," Dan said. "You didn't believe us."

Charli felt as if she were watching a play. The stage was the Crandalls' porch, and the actors, her beloved Aunt Lilly and Uncle Will, were playing unfamiliar, painful roles.

"We shouldn't be watching this," Rona murmured, but nobody moved. Even the twins were silent.

Then, as suddenly as it had begun, the conversation ended. Well, it hadn't been a real conversation, Charli decided. Uncle Will had nodded a few times, but he hadn't said a word. When Aunt Lilly went into the house, he slumped heavily on the porch swing and ran his fingers through his mop of gray hair.

"Poor Dad," Dan said, and Charli glanced up at him in surprise. Lately he'd been angry with Uncle Will all the time, but now he sounded sorry for him. "Come on, kids. I guess we can go home now."

Charli wanted desperately to go with them, but she didn't dare. "It's none of our business," Ray would say, even though he'd been as curious as she was about what was happening. She watched as the twins climbed into the swing and Uncle Will took Mickey on his lap. Dan leaned against the porch railing. It is, too, our business,

Charli thought. She had always been a part of what happened to the Crandalls.

"Look, he's beckoning!" she exclaimed. "Let's go. Please!"

To her surprise, Ray didn't argue.

"Got something to tell you," Uncle Will said when they had joined him on the porch. "Maybe it'll be a relief to you after that scare this afternoon, but still it's a big disappointment." He smiled sadly at Charli. "You and Sophia have put in a lot of work, but I have to tell you there isn't going to be a Crandalls' Castle."

They stared at him.

"But you've bought the place, Dad," Dan said. "All that money!"

"Most of our savings," Uncle Will admitted. "It would probably take everything we have before it'd be ready for paying guests. I've spent the day talking to people I thought would want to invest, but so far nobody's interested."

Charli looked sideways at Ray. If he said "I told you so!" she'd never forgive him.

"But that's not the reason I'm quitting," Uncle Will said. "Money isn't everything, you know. I'd have figured out a way. . . ." He glanced toward the sagging screen door. "It's Lilly. She doesn't want any of our family to go inside the place again. Including me! She says she's never insisted on having her way before, which is true, but she's insisting now. And I have to respect that. She's a wonderful woman."

"Amen to that," Ray said. "Did she tell you what scared her off?" He cocked his head at Charli. "We're having a little trouble finding out."

"There's a haunted bedroom," Uncle Will said. "I've always said a ghost would be an advantage in a bed-and-breakfast, but Lilly says no. She says Mickey got up there and was nearly suffocated. If it hadn't been for Sophia—she guessed where he was so they got there in time. . . ."

Ray sighed and gave up. "Where *is* Sophia?" he asked. "It sounds as if she deserves congratulations."

"I'll get her," Charli offered quickly. She hurried inside and up the stairs, eager to get away from Uncle Will's disappointment. She didn't want him to know his bad news had made her feel absolutely wonderful.

She knocked on the door of the catchall room, and Sophia said, "Come in," in a voice as sad as Uncle Will's.

The room had changed. Boxes had been

pushed under the bed or stacked in a corner, and white curtains tied back with blue ribbons matched the quilt on the bed. Sophia sat on the side of the bed writing in a book.

"What's that?" Charli asked, suddenly shy. "A diary?"

She half-expected to be told it was private business, but Sophia just shrugged.

"Sort of," she said briefly. "Something to talk to."

"But you have real people to talk to," Charli protested. "You have Aunt Lilly and Uncle Will and Dan and—you could talk to me if you wanted to."

"Maybe," Sophia said slowly. "But I say the wrong things. People think you're weird if you know things before they happen."

Charli wondered how many more surprises this day could hold. Smart, confident Sophia actually worried about how other people felt about her!

"Well, I might have thought that," she admitted. "Just at first, I mean. But you saved Mickey's life, so nobody's going to call you weird now."

Sophia closed her book and looked up. Her eyes were red. "It doesn't matter anyway," she said. "I'll be leaving here soon."

Charli frowned. "You're leaving? Are you sure?"

"I know because of Lilly," Sophia replied with a touch of her old impatience. "Haven't you noticed how quiet she's been since we got back from Madison? I came to Wisconsin in the first place because my great-grandmother was here. Now that she's gone, I'll have to go back to California."

That didn't make sense to Charli. "You'd better come downstairs," she said finally. "Everyone wants to thank you for saving Mickey." Then she remembered Uncle Will's big news. "Uncle Will isn't going to have a Crandalls' Castle after all," she announced. "Aunt Lilly won't let him."

That, she was pleased to see, made Sophia smile.

The scene on the front porch was pretty much as she'd left it. The twins had moved to the steps with their cars, and Rona was cuddling Mickey. No one was talking. Uncle Will looked close to tears, but his face lit up when he saw Sophia.

"We've got a lot to thank you for, Sophia," he said huskily. "Lilly says you were the only one who guessed where the kids had gone."

"She didn't guess, she *knew*," Charli said proudly. "She knows things before they happen." She looked at Ray when she said it, daring him to argue.

"I don't see how—" he began, but Sophia didn't wait for him to finish. "Neither do I," she said simply. "But sometimes it just happens."

Silence returned, except for the noise of the racing-car drivers on the steps.

"I suppose Charli told you about the Castle," Uncle Will said dejectedly. "I know you're disappointed, too—you girls have worked hard."

"Listen, Will," Ray said suddenly, "I don't understand what happened today, and I'm beginning to think I never will, but whatever, it's probably for the best."

Charli scowled at him. He was going to say it. He was actually going to say "I told you so!"

"You own the land," Ray went on. "If you tear down that wreck of a house, you'll have a pile of pretty good lumber to work with. Build something else there—something really useful. If you do, it'll be a lot easier to find investors to help."

Uncle Will stared at him.

"Come up with a good idea," Ray went on, "and I might be glad to invest in it myself."

Uncle Will stood up, his eyes bright. "You mean it? You mean you'd be interested in—in Crandalls' Castle Hotel?"

Ray shook his head. "Way too big," he said. "Too grand. Too much money."

"How about Crandalls' Castle Motel?"

Ray shook his head again. "I was thinking of something really practical for all the tourists who'll be coming this way. How about a Laundromat?"

Uncle Will looked stunned. "A—a Laundromat?" He thought about it, while Charli held her breath. Then he snapped his fingers. "I've got it!" he exclaimed. "Crandalls' Castle of Clean Clothes." His eyes sparkled and he reached over to shake Ray's hand. "We'll have a play area for kids and a coffee corner and maybe a lending library and . . ."

They were all laughing by that time and Charli was dizzy with pleasure. Instead of making Uncle Will feel worse, Ray had come up with a way to make him happy again. It was unbelievable. Uncle Will was smiling, and it was her blunt, no-nonsense, wonderful stepfather who had done it.

"Lemonade, anyone?"

Aunt Lilly appeared at the door, carrying a

tray of glasses. Dan hurried to open the screen for her, and Charli and Sophia passed the glasses around.

"Wait'll I tell you the news, Lilly!" Uncle Will exclaimed. "You'll love it!"

Aunt Lilly settled on the swing next to him. She was herself again, smiling contentedly at them all. "I'm sure I will," she said. "You all look so happy—except our Sophia."

"I'm okay," Sophia said quickly. "Honest!"

Charli peeled a scrap of paper off the bottom of a glass and handed the lemonade to Dan. She was about to drop the paper back onto the tray when Aunt Lilly stopped her.

"Read that, Charli," she urged. "Read it out loud. It's a telephone message Dan left on the kitchen counter. I didn't notice it until just now."

Charli smoothed the sticky note. "It says, 'Rita called.' Who's Rita?"

"She's a social worker in Madison," Sophia said in a dull voice. "She was at the funeral."

"Read the rest," Aunt Lilly said. She was still smiling but now there were tears on her cheeks.

"It says, 'All fine with Sacramento if it's fine with you. Tell Sophia.'" Charli studied the words. "That means she doesn't have to go back to California, right?"

"That's right," Aunt Lilly said. "We hoped she could stay right here with us, but Rita wasn't sure. She's been checking into it."

"Go back?" Ray repeated indignantly. "Why in the world would she want to go back?"

"I didn't!" Sophia exclaimed. "I don't!"

"But you said you were going," Charli said. "You said you'd have to. I thought it was one of those things you *knew*."

Sophia's cheeks were pink and her voice shook. "I thought so, too," she said softly. "But I was wrong."